The Healing Reunion

Julie Kilpatrick

ISBN: 0615784615
ISBN-13: 9780615784618

This book is dedicated to my wonderful husband, Jimmy. I am so grateful for your endless love and support throughout this journey. Thank you for always listening to my ideas and believing in me.

1972
Virginia Beach, VA

Gary Stokes listens to the rain pelting the ambulance roof. As the vehicle slows to a stop, he squeezes Marcie's limp hand.

"We're here Sweet Pea."

Her face twitches.

The double door opens. "Did you reach my wife?"

"Yes, Sir. She knows you're here. Your daughter's vitals are stable, but that bump needs to be looked at. She's a lucky girl."

It's more than luck. Did God answer his prayers? Is it a miracle?

As they unload the stretcher, Gary's eyes catch on the puka necklace around her tiny arm. It was a gift from the lifeguard.

Once inside, the medical staff whisks her away. He closes his eyes.

"Gary?"

There she stands. The love of his life, her eyes franticly looking for answers.

"What happened? Is she going to be okay?"

He wraps his arms around her. "Yes, she'll be fine."

After a moment, she pulls away.

"How could you let this happen?"

"I'm sorry. I'm really sorry."

He reaches for her again and is met with folded arms.

"Gary, don't. We'll talk later."

The next hours seem a blur. When the hospital finally releases their little girl, Gary sighs. *She's going to be okay.*

***

Early the next morning, he sticks to his usual routine, waking before sunrise. Gloria doesn't trust him anymore and he must fix that. He also wants to have a talk with God, something he hasn't done since he was a boy.

He throws on his jogging attire, grabs a piece of paper and pen, and writes the one Bible verse stuck in his memory. John 3:16. He whispers as he writes, "For God so loved the world that he gave his only begotten son that whosoever believeth in him should not perish, but have everlasting life."

He lists the words *prayer*, *church*, and *God*, and after folding it, sticks the paper in his shorts' pocket. He is about to leave when he hears a creak in the hallway. A few seconds later, Gloria appears.

"Going for a jog?"

"Yep. Just need to clear my head. We'll talk when I get back?"

"I don't even know what to say to you. My only child could have died."

"I know. She's my child too. It was an accident."

"What happened? You stayed in the water when it was storming? Who does that? Especially with a child?"

"Gloria, it happened so fast. The storm came out of nowhere."

"It didn't come out of nowhere. You knew it was going to storm. We talked about it, remember? I told you I didn't think you should go. I warned you. You get so caught up in being the *fun* one, that you forget you're the parent."

"Aww come on. That's not fair. One minute the sky was clear and the next minute it wasn't."

"You said you would keep her safe."

"I know."

"You promised me she would be okay. You promised me." Her voice cracks, inclining him to pull her close to him.

"I will never forgive myself. Don't you know that? I will never do anything like that again."

She pulls away, but this time grabs his hands.

"I believe you. And...I forgive you."

She returns to their bedroom as Gary stretches his legs. His daughter shouldn't be alive. She was under the water too long.

When he's ready, he peeks in the bedroom. Marcie is curled in a fetal position nestled next to Gloria's chest. He blows kisses and leaves the house.

Hitting the pavement full force, he's ready to work out the unanswered clutter in his mind. The storm that battered the area the day before left the city like an unwanted guest and a lukewarm breeze resides now.

He reaches a steady gait, his breathing in rhythm with his steps, and replays the previous day's events. He should have listened to his wife and the weather forecast. He shouldn't have given in to Marcie's pleading to swim in the ocean with the storm approaching. And that is the hardest thing for him—always wanting to give in to Marcie.

He speeds up as the guilt eats at him. His heartbeat is no longer in sync with the rest of his body. His heart is broken. He's been away from God too long and this is his wake-up call.

Taking advantage of the earliness of the morning, he runs with freedom, void of bicycles, baby carriages, or people. At each corner, he slows slightly, glancing each way before jogging across the street.

Thinking of the Bible verse scribbled in his pocket, he mumbles it between breaths.

"For God so loved the world." That means him. God loves him.

"He gave his only begotten son that whosoever believeth in Him." He believes. His sins are forgiven.

"Shall not perish but have everlasting life." A calm falls over him. He is on the edge of turning around his life. He can feel it.

The thought settles in as he reaches his block. He repeats his glancing routine and proceeds to cross the street. It's still dark and although he didn't see the reckless car careening out of control, the last sounds he hears are brakes screeching and tires squealing. And a scream.

Chapter 1
~Marcie~

*T*he remnant of eternal wedded bliss suffocates Marcie's finger. Attempts to twist off the band of her broken marriage only ends up stirring the embers of unresolved feelings.

Poor Seth. He never expected the baggage from her scattered past, and he certainly didn't deserve the wreckage it caused. Blame fell on her, solely.

The room spins. Or maybe it's the pain pills taunting her brain. They usually ease her knee pain, but today is different. She's certain that the years of pounding the pavement, chasing her personal best, brought her to the inevitable suffering at forty. She just didn't plan that her new silent partner would affect her marriage.

Straightening her skirt in the mirror, she considers skipping church. Not that she is a regular anyway. If those daily do-gooders and weekly tithers really got to know her they'd probably feel inclined to take her out to the parking lot and cast stones until she bled.

She shifts her gaze. Bloodshot eyes stare back. *Will anyone suspect?*

With her lap-top open from a night of chatting and surfing, she struggles to recall her keyboard clicks. Her desk, piled with empty containers, power drink bottles, and a soon-to-be-finalized divorce decree paper, seems messier than she remembers. Hopefully she didn't do anything stupid.

After smacking the computer closed, she attempts to push the drawer in, but it stops abruptly. Papers, clips, and pencils block her hand until she grazes the culprit. Even before she sees it, she already recognizes the feel of the worn plastic that holds a folded paper and puka-shell necklace. Instantly, she fights the urge to take the trip down memory lane, certain she will ball her eyes out. But giving into the sweet innocence of childhood is worth the bitter she will feel later. She lets the memory flood her brain.

***

1972

"Marcie, you're as fast as the wind."

Even at six she knew her dad was her biggest fan. And that same year she fell in love with running.

"You're as fast as the wind if you put your mind to it. It's a breee-eeeze!" He always made a zooming sound, which would set off her giggling. It didn't matter that she'd heard it a million times.

During the summer months, they made a habit of hopping into his '67 blue convertible Volkswagen and driving to the beach. Their routine was always the same– throwing their towels, lunch cooler, and blanket on the sand at their favorite weekend spot, before racing to see who would touch the frigid water first. That was always followed by digging for sand dollars and fiddler crabs, eating PB&J sandwiches, and burying her father in the sand.

But nothing compared to running up and down the beach. He always teased her, grabbing her sun hat or flip-flops, pretending to throw them in the ocean. Just at the point she would catch him, he would take off like a jet and they lost themselves in an imaginary world of deep-sea diving, mermaids, and treasures.

One August Saturday morning, when the weather reached record-breaking temperatures, and the jellyfish made their presence known, she asked if she could bring her new raft. Her promise to care for it along with her deep-crater smile cinched the deal.

Her mom was placing their lunch in the canvas bag when she said, "Gary, you think you should go today? Newspaper's calling for strong winds and rain this afternoon."

"I will make sure our precious daughter is safe, I promise." And he gently kissed her and declared, "Even though we have a bounty of treasure to hunt, we won't stay long!"

Once they made it to the beach, they moved quickly across the hot sand, beach gear in tow, along with the raft. They weaved through the waves of people, not wasting any time to find a spot, and stripped down to their bathing suits.

Marcie dragged the raft and copied her father's foot imprints in the sand. Passing the lifeguard stand, she glanced up and the lifeguard winked at her. She smiled and admired his puka-shelled necklace.

When they reached the water, her dad hesitated.

"What's wrong, Daddy?"

"Well, Sweet Pea, those waves are looking mighty big. I think we need to stay closer to the shore today."

Her heart dropped. With school just around the corner, it was her last day to show how her big girl kicks improved.

"Please, Daddy. We'll be fast… please??"

"I don't know."

"*Pleeeeeease.*"

He gave in. He picked her up with the raft, and headed to the water. "We'll go in for a little bit but you have to listen to me really good, okay? And when it's time to get out, no pouting."

"You're the best!"

They waded through the water until it hit her father's waistline. After she climbed onto the raft, he held onto the rope while she bobbed up and down like a buoy out at sea. She squealed with delight.

They didn't notice right away the current pushed them so far that the lifeguard wasn't in view. Marcie was too busy laughing at the large waves which almost bounced her off the raft. Her father seemed concerned.

"Sweet Pea, we need to get out. I'm gonna need you to hold on with both your hands and wrap your legs around the raft, okay? I need to have both my hands to pull."

Only moments later, two significant things happened. A shrill whistle piped in the air, causing her dad to look in the sound's direction. At the same time, a large wave towered over them like a ferocious dragon ready to devour its prey.

By the time her dad had an inkling of what was happening, it was too late. The colossal wave crashed down with no remorse. They were pulled apart and she was tossed into the water, and dragged mercilessly toward the ocean's floor. Her head slammed into the shell-filled sand and her body spun out of control. The blow left her terrified as her arms and legs turned to wet noodles. Water rammed its way into every crevice of her body as if the ocean was having a snack. Too weak and battered to do anything, she slowly descended and hit the bottom again.

***

Marcie's hand aches from the tight grip on the necklace. She releases it to see tiny indentations on her palm.

Shaken, she begins to return the necklace to the bag, but instead hooks it around her neck. The piece of paper, still in the plastic, will be conquered another day. One step at a time.

With newfound courage, she opens her laptop. Immediately, her Facebook account appears and a conversation with Andrea Fowler pops up. Andrea Fowler? *Who is Andrea Fowler and why am I chatting with her?*

The dialogue seems scattered but it doesn't take long to realize Andrea is her childhood friend, Andrea Fishkin.

Andrea Fowler,
June 28, 2012 10:30 am
Hello Marcie—I don't know how well you remember me from Jefferson elementary. You might remember my fun last name? You had some fond ways of referring to it that made me laugh. Unlike the boys that made fun of me. BTW-remember Christopher Fowler? It's no coincidence we have the same last name. I married him. Isn't that crazy? We've been married since high school and have 2 daughters, Reese (20) and Rochelle (15). I'm still in Norfolk. How about you? Tell me what's going on when you have a sec.

Marcie Stokes Griffin
August 12, 2012 10:30 pm

Hi Andrea. Sorry to delay. Still in the area too - crazy huh? I definitly member you. You helped me read. What was the name of the other girl... Charlie? Have you heard from her????

She bites her lip, cringing. She sounds like an idiot.

Andrea Fowler
August 12, 2012 10:35 pm
Yes, Charlie Baldwin. She was kind of quiet but we took care of that didn't we? Remember what we called ourselves? The 3 stooges! I think that I was Moe, you were Curly and she was Larry. We would hang at my house and you would plan these elaborate slapstick routines in our backyard. Remember the bull fighter one? We were such dorks! I've got a pic of our class. I'll post it in a few minutes. See if you recognize everyone.

Marcie Stokes Griffin
August 12, 2012 10:45 pm
Ok I'll see if I can find her. Its really good talking to you.

Andrea Fowler
August 12, 2012 11:30 pm
So I see you're a night owl too. As promised, here's our first grade class. Found this last week going through my mother's things. There are a bunch of pictures I hadn't seen in thirty years. Look at Christopher. Boy, has he gotten better looking! Remember Charlie's grandfather fixed her hair and she hated it and was crying that whole morning until picture time? You tried cheering her up. Were you able to find her?

Marcie Stokes Griffin
August 12, 2012 11:36 pm
I found a Charlie Baldwin but the pic was a dog- I mean she's not a dog I mean that pictur is a dog you know what I mean I'll see if she respond or not

She can't read any more of the muddled writing. Instead, she grabs her Bible and takes off. Whether they'll be eager to see her or not, she will be making an appearance at church.

Chapter 2
~Charlie~

Clock-watching is Charlie's faithful nemesis. Nights repeat an ensemble of tossing and turning, stretching muscles, and desperate prayers. And as always, three-year-old Jake, her devoted Jack Russell, sleeps soundly underneath the covers, no concern for her dilemma.

When menopause crept into her life, her trips to Dr. Shepherd increased, hoping to find the perfect remedies to combat hot flashes, night sweats, and the worst case of insomnia she'd ever experienced. And while her personal summers improved, ever so slightly, the sleeplessness had made itself at home.

She tried every relief known to woman, from removing all traces of light to hot baths laced with soothing bath oils. She even bought a sleep mask with matching earplugs, but quickly ditched them when

Jake growled at her. They had to go.

Most nights, when she reached the breaking point, she resorted to joining millions of other nocturnal creatures on chatrooms and discussion boards. But this night she tries desperately not to give in to the voices begging her to talk to them.

Instead, she replays her last appointment two days ago when Dr. Shepherd asked if she was under a lot of stress.

"Charlie, you know stress can bring on these symptoms more frequently."

Keenly aware her stress levels bring out the worst of her episodes, she didn't want to go into details of what was truly bothering her. Sadly, even her doctor's wisdom couldn't knock her out of her rut.

Most of it involves work at the Eastside Service Center where she'd served as a social worker for over ten years. They recently experienced severe cutbacks. When two of the Center's social workers lost their jobs, her caseload grew instantly from fifteen to twenty active investigations. An exhausting number even for a veteran as herself. The fact that her families would get even less of her time and energy consumed her. Her one consolation—she still has a job.

To make matters worse, her work hours leave only a tiny window to spend with Lawrence, her second conundrum. Although a solid partner when it comes to relationship material, he seems to only have marriage on his mind. It doesn't help that he's beyond expectations in the sweet and loyal categories, making him hard to resist. But her dog also fits that bill, and he requires much less of her.

Lately, his matrimony drivel spills into every conversation. The more he speaks the 'M' word, the more she wonders why she is with a man ten years her junior.

She couldn't tell Dr. Shepherd all of that though. And she certainly couldn't tell her about their encounter before her last appointment.

That night she tried resisting his insistence on coming over, but his promise of bringing ice cream and toppings won out. She couldn't pass on the temptation. Besides, he said he had something important to tell her.

He arrived on time as usual. In contrast to him, she would most likely be late to her own funeral. Luckily, he found out early in the relationship, and kept his thoughts to himself on the subject.

The ice cream was barely scooped out of the container and into the bowls when he revealed his agenda. "So, are you ready for the news?"

"What news?"

He squirted chocolate on their scoops.

"I found a venue for our wedding."

She squinted as if blinded by his words.

"Aren't you putting the cart before the horse? I haven't even said, *yes* yet."

He topped each dish with nuts.

"You will."

She looked away from her Sicilian catch, wondering at what ripe age he mastered the art of charm. He was very convincing. When she finally spoke, her words were rushed.

"Why the urgency? I'm not going anywhere. I want to be with you. Matter of fact, I love spending time with you. I just don't want to get married right now. I thought we were on the same page."

Never one to beat around the bush, he replied, "What are you waiting for? Some knight in shining armor? I can be that if it matters. I don't get you. We aren't getting any younger."

She stifled the laugh pulling at the bit; she was the one fast approaching a half–century, not him. Instead, she spooned a dollop of whipped cream onto the nuts and handed him the bowl.

"Maybe I am afraid of commitment. Do you blame me? Half of marriages end in divorce. I see it every day I go to work. How do we know that ours won't be the same? Why ruin a good thing?"

"How will marrying ruin anything? Ours doesn't have to be defined by what's trending today. We don't have to be the norm. Besides, you said your grandparents were married for years."

He placed his bowl down and reached for her hand.

"Ours can last the rest of our lives."

Instead of accepting it, she whispered, "Like yours did?"

She couldn't ignore his fifteen-year marriage to his first wife. They were only divorced a year before she met him.

"You know she left me."

"Right. Do you see where that might even be worse to me? You took your vows seriously, you said, and tried to make it work. She was the one done with your marriage. Did you all of a sudden fall out of love with her? How do I know that you don't have feelings for her still?"

"I told you that things had been bad between us for a while. And, yes, I did want to work it out because of my Christian faith, but I couldn't force her to stay with me. That doesn't mean I can't love you."

Before she could stop herself, she answered, "I'm not in love with you."

His face turned grim. No doubt, her words pierced his heart, and she contemplated taking them back. The spark of glimmering hope fled and he looked defeated. She hadn't meant to hurt him, but that's what she seemed to do best. Like a match, if people got too close they were likely to get burned.

He set the ice cream bowl on the counter and washed his hands in the sink. As he dried them he said, "I hope you find what you're looking for, Charlie." With that he left and she was alone with her lie.

***

Thinking of the ice cream episode, Charlie is suddenly hungry. She stuffs her feet into her favorite fuzzy slippers and throws on her worn robe. Jake feigns interest as he stretches deeply, bottom up. She smiles at his comedy relief before he burrows back into the covers.

Padding into the kitchen, she contemplates rustling up a snack. Her love for cooking has taken a backseat to everything else, and she finds herself dining on fast food and frozen dinners. She opens the refrigerator door, hoping for inspiration to create something of substance. The sparse vessel yields condiments, over-ripe produce, and half a quart of outdated milk. Maybe the pantry is more promising.

Much to her relief, she sees her tried-and-true Oreos on the top shelf and snatches the treats as if they will disappear before she can indulge in them. Along with a glass of milk and her laptop, she has the perfect late night trifecta.

As she munches, she thinks of her grandfather. On Friday nights when she was little, Poppy would allow her to stay up until midnight and they would play checkers or chess and dunk Oreos in milk. His milk mustache always made her laugh as he taught her life strategies for playing games and eating Oreos.

She suddenly aches for her grandfather's sound advice, even though lately he delves less advice and instead seems to be asking more questions.

She hates traveling the road of self-pity but as she stares at her hands, which recently earned their first age spots, it's hard not to feel sad. These are the hands of a middle-aged woman still living by herself with her dog. Who would take care of her if she became ill like Poppy?

Poppy would certainly chide her for feeling sorry for herself. "*Feeling sorry for yourself is not only a waste of energy but the worst habit you could have,*" rings in her ears. Someone famous quoted it. Curiously, she grabs her laptop on the counter to find the answer but stops short at the open Facebook screen.

Chapter 3
~Andrea~

*T*he freshly cut lawn and scattered rosebushes give Andrea a pinch of gratification. Dirt and sweat has finally paid off this year. Now she's certain Chris will finally shut up about maintaining it himself. She relishes the view—*and the thought*— for a moment, before opening the doors to the patio.

Breathing in the warm end-of-summer air, she admires the perfectly pruned trees and shrubs that decorate the yard. The large magnolia, whose branches dangle gracefully over the pond, is still her favorite.

She steps toward the tempting crystal-clear pool. A quick dip is in order. That is until she notices the patio furniture out of place. Having just straightened up the day before, she wonders which daughter rearranged during the night. The thought almost swings her mood, but she catches it off guard with a controlled set of deep breaths. Relaxing once again, she is determined not to have the morning ruined by their lack of respect. While at the age of cleaning up after themselves, she recognizes they have not picked up her zeal for tidiness.

When everything is returned to its proper place, she concludes it had to be her youngest, Rochelle. Her teenaged rebellion has recently stepped up a notch. As she stoops to pluck the weeds vying for the flower bed with the marigolds, she imagines the confrontation. It will most likely end with Rochelle running to her room and Chris looking at her as if she's the worst mother in the world. Lately, they aren't seeing eye-to-eye, especially when it comes to her.

Her cell is ringing as she steps inside.

"Andrea?"

"Chris."

"Well, it's good we still remember each other's names."

His attempt at small talk and humor annoys her. Besides, her schedule is too full to waste frivolously.

"What do you need?"

"Just wanted to see what you had planned for dinner. With the girls going out, thought I'd give you a little break. I can grill some steaks."

"That's not necessary. I can have it ready when you get home."

"I'd like to do this for you. You never take a break. And I really want to make up for—"

"You don't owe me anything, Chris. Look, I need to go. We'll talk later."

"Fine. I'll see you later. I love you." He sounds exasperated. To get him off the phone, she replies hastily, "You too."

She shoves the conversation in her mind's junk drawer, along with all of the other similar ones. It makes it easier to tackle the day's agenda which includes a very promising video teleconference. By ten o'clock, she has to be ready to present her new marketing ideas to *All Fed Up*.

Pouring her first coffee of the day, she dissects Chris's phone call. His real reason for calling. To an outsider, it would surely sound innocent enough. But to Andrea, it is plain odd he feels the need to call her several times a day. As if he doesn't trust her. It doesn't make sense. After all, he's the one with the roaming eye.

After a few sips, she tackles the dishes, dusting, laundry and heads to the closet for the vacuum when her phone rings. Chris. Again. *What is wrong with him?* She clicks it to silent and continues her chores. Once satisfied, she heads to the shower, still miffed at his persistence.

As the hot water pelts her, she relaxes and considers that maybe his intentions are innocent. She does have to admit her personality is a little intense. But what does he expect? He knows she was raised in a dysfunctional family or what she likes to call the *Fishkin loony bin*. She even admitted, on their second date, she had some obsessive compulsive traits. Why now the sudden need to smother her?

She steps out, grabs her gold towel, and in an attempt to get Chris out of her mind, she replays the recent communication with her long-lost childhood friend, Marcie. They were inseparable for years in elementary school, but silent decades divided the friendship. Now she questions the need for her to contact her old friend, wondering where it will lead once they cover family, career and home.

She breathes in the towel's lavender scent, amused at her tomboy transition to Suzie Homemaker over the years. Marcie will have a hard time recognizing her.

With only half-hour to spare until her meeting, she throws on her blouse and slacks, brushes on makeup, professional but not overdone, and combs through her short hair. After a dab of red gloss, she dashes downstairs to her office, clicks on the computer's camera and adjusts it until it focuses on her.

While waiting, she glances at her outdated executive chair and mahogany bookshelf with the vintage porcelain Lladros from her mother's estate. Once her business picks up, replacing all of the junk will be first priority.

She opens her portfolio link and in doing so, she notices a friend request on her Facebook account. Charlie Baldwin. She smirks at the picture of a big-eared white and brown dog. He's cute but she can't understand why someone would want that as a profile picture.

Accepting the friend request, she closes out the page, and connects to the *All Fed Up* meeting, eager to share with the editors the latest food blog and photos for their magazine. As she waits, a childhood event comes to mind.

***

1972

The laughter came from every direction, schoolboys taunting her as if she were trash.

"Andrea Fishkin… Andrea Fishkin… if she can't do it, Andrea's fish can!" And then another wave of laughter.

Her anger boiled like a cauldron's brew. If they weren't careful it would spew like a volcano. She lunged at them with fists.

"Shut up! Shut up!"

One particular brave boy ran by, yanking her hair as he yelled, "What's that smell? It's Andrea's fish can. Gross!"

On that early Indian summer morning, there were two things the fair-haired boy had not anticipated during recess—Andrea's anger and leg speed. Had he anticipated those things he might have thought twice about getting near, because within seconds, she had a tight grip on his cotton shirt. It was enough to rip it down the middle. He jerked backwards and fell to the ground.

With no chance of a counterattack, the boy put his hands up in defense as she straddled him, pinning his body down with her legs, pummeling his head with her fists. Immediately cheers and screams fill the air as children ran from all areas of the playground to see the commotion.

"Fight! Fight! Fight!"

Some resorted to pushing and shoving in order to get a better view and within a matter of minutes more fights broke out.

By the time the teachers caught on to the chaos, World War III had erupted at Jefferson Elementary. Most of the girls and boys returned to class right away, but a few playground war casualties stayed behind, babying their wounds, tears streaming down their faces.

Andrea stood tall, admiring her creation. Not that she wanted to cause suffering, she only wanted to stand up for herself. She stared fiercely until the art teacher grabbed her by the arm, spinning her dizzy.

"Andrea, did you start this? Let's go to the principal's office."

While most kids usually cried at the threat of the principal's office, she strutted proudly, chin up, arms crossed, as she was steered through the aftermath of her rage.

***

The phone startles her. The number doesn't look familiar.

"Hello."

"Andrea? This is Callie Barton. Maggie Ryan's assistant at *All Fed Up.*"

"Oh, yes, I remember. How are you?"

"Fine, thank you. Sorry to change plans at the last minute but Ms. Ryan needs to reschedule the meeting. She's a little under the weather."

"I'm sorry to hear that." Andrea tries not to reveal her disappointment.

"Rest assured, Ms. Ryan is very interested in what you have to show us and wants to reschedule early next week."

"That sounds fine. Please send her my regards."

"I will. Again, I apologize. And I'll be calling you soon."

"Thank you."

In one fowl swoop, days of preparing layouts, writing short briefs, and editing over and over seems for naught. Rolling her eyes, she closes her files, stopping short of turning off the monitor when she notices her Facebook account again. A highlighted message from Charlie grabs her attention.

Charlie Baldwin
August 14, 2012 9:00 am
Marcie & Andrea —This is such a great blast from the past. I can't believe we are connecting after so many years! I've been in Florida

for the last 20 years and am a social worker. I had such fond memories of our childhood together. Tell me what's going on with both of you.

Good ol' Charlie. Innocent as Bambi.

Andrea studies her manicured nails, painted to professional perfection. She doesn't expect anything less from herself. She pictures Charlie's accepting smile at her prissiness. Charlie is accepting of everything and everyone. Well, at least she used to be. Andrea grimaces. Will she still accept her once she got to know her again? She refills her coffee before responding.

Andrea Fowler
August 14, 2012 9:42 am
Hello Ladies – It really is wonderful catching up. I still can't believe it. Charlie, you were so mature and well behaved and Marcie you were so funny. Remember how the three of us met at my mother's studio?

Andrea stops typing and recalls the exact moment she met Marcie.

***

1972

After causing the playground riot, Andrea played out her three-day-suspension at her mother's dreaded dance studio. Next to sharing a room with her siblings, it was the worst punishment ever. Watching girls bouncing around in their leotards annoyed her.

She made the best of her punishment, and listened to her mother's warning to remain in the small office space in the back.

The first day she snooped about, curious of the dance memorabilia. Portraits of children posing in their ballet apparel hung on every wall. Trophies were lined up proudly on almost every shelf. A few dance uniforms were tossed about but most hung on a rack behind a desk piled with paperwork.

A photo with several girls interests her. A skinny curly-haired blond stood out from the rest. The girl's smile stretched ear-to-ear, revealing a huge gap in her mouth where two front teeth were missing. She immediately recognized Marcie, the girl she would be helping with her homework.

"Andrea, I want you to meet someone."

Her mother tapped her shoulder.

"This is Marcie. I was telling you about her. You may have remembered seeing her before. She's going to work on her homework for a little bit before dance class. I know you'll have no problem helping her if she needs it."

Marcie waved. "Hi."

"Hi. What do you need help with?"

Marcie shrugged, and peered at Andrea's mother opening her satchel. Her mother cleared her desk to make room and within a few minutes the two were alone.

Neither said anything for a while until Andrea asked, "Are you dumb?"

"No. Are you?"

"No. Why do you need help then?"

Marcie shrugged again.

She studied Marcie another minute and then noticed the shells around her neck. "I like your necklace."

"Thank you."

"I beat up a boy," Andrea said proudly.

"My daddy died."

At that moment, Andrea knew they would be good friends.

Chapter 4
~Marcie~

*T*he sound of elliptical machines and treadmills whir in the mid-morning hours at the gym that Marcie calls second home. As the early risers work their bodies to music, she inspects the few empty machines, wiping here and there, and sizes up the morning personalities. Thirty percent hardcore fitness nuts with bulging biceps and zero to two percent body fat. Thirty percent beginners, poor to fair shape trying to figure out the machines. Forty percent regulars trying to keep a healthy lifestyle. The usual population.

"Hey, Marcie. What time's your first appointment?"

Anthony is behind her carrying a clipboard and stopwatch.

"My first canceled. Second doesn't come for another hour. Why?" She sensed a favor coming her way.

"Maria's coming in fifteen minutes. Thought you could help me out."

"Maria? The one that looks like a poodle on steroids?" .

Anthony laughed. "You're crazy. Yeah, that's the one."

"Am I lying? I swear she got stuck in the seventies!"

"You're right. Crazy hair. Anyway, think you can help me out?"

"Everything okay?"

"Yeah. Just gotta run an errand."

She cringes as he drops his head and says, "You know I'll make it worth your while,"

Deep in her gut she hears '*your sin will find you out*'.

"I don't need you to make it worth my while. I was going to help you anyway."

"Appreciate it." He leans in and whispers, "Check our spot. Got something for you."

She walks away as if she doesn't hear.

Her client's assessment is uneventful. After taking measurements, discussing her fitness plan, and instructing her on a few machines, Marcie gives her a thumbs up while secretly envying the older woman's will to take care of herself in a clean way.

As the woman walks away, Marcie feels her knee throb. She rubs the swollen kneecap until she can't stand it anymore and heads to the locker room for her bandage.

While wrapping it, she considers Anthony's enticing offer. She's still thinking about it when she stops at the sink to wash her hands. At least her reflection is better than the other night.

Pastor Sinclair's sermon hit her hard. At one point, she was certain he was speaking directly to her, as if he had celestial x-ray vision eyes that could see to her soul.

The pain throbs on like a freight train. Perhaps she'll just have one. She limps over to the couch backed up to the wall.

Her watch keeps perfect time and she has only a few minutes until the next client. Should she ditch the mission?

The door opens. She immediately sits down as a slim girl enters, smiles, and goes to a stall. Marcie lets out a deep breath.

I'm not going to make it today. Lord, help me.

She waits for a sign of healing.

Moments later, the girl opens the door and looks at Marcie.

"You okay?"

Marcie nods. *Okay this is it. This is your moment to walk out and get back to work.*

"Well, have a good day!"

And she's gone, leaving Marcie alone with her misery.

Surrendering, she pulls herself up, winces, and walks to the couch's back corner. Her hand slides down the back until she feels the torn flap. She flips the fabric and in an instant, finds what she is looking for and pulls it out. Six pills wrapped in plastic wrap, courtesy of Anthony. After popping one in her mouth, she leaves the bathroom to meet her next client.

***

"So here's what I think."

Anthony smirks as he pulls up a chair in the staff break room.

Marcie continues eating her afternoon nutrition bar, attempting to ignore him.

"Look, I got a proposition for you."

She looks at her watch. "Look, Anthony, I'm looking to leave here in an hour. Besides, you're gonna get fired if you don't watch out."

"You might be right, but just chill for a minute. You like dough, right? You want to earn a little extra?"

She swigs her bottled water. "If this is illegal, I'm out."

Anthony snorts. "No, I promise. It's a nutritional supplement. Nothing but the best vitamins and minerals. You'll be helping people replenish what their bodies are missing. I know you like to help people."

"I don't want any part of it, so talk to the hand."

"You're so old school. *'Talk to the hand.'*" He laughs until he points to her neck. "Where'd you get that?"

She touches the puka-shells.

"I've had this awhile. I found it recently in my drawer."

"Oh. No, no, no, no… that is weak. Who wears that crap? You need something fancy. Now if you want to buy some real jewelry, I'm telling you I've got a deal for you."

Fed up with his nonsense, she finishes her snack, throws away the trash, and walks toward the door. He grabs her arm.

"Hold on. Don't leave. I'll stop buggin' you. I promise. Sit down for a minute. I want to talk to you about something."

Shaken by his sudden distress, she returns to her seat. She feels lightheaded anyway, not certain if it's Anthony's babble, her blood pressure, or the effects of the medication.

"What?"

"So who gave you that?" This time he touches her necklace, making her feel uneasy. She leans back.

"That's not what you were going to ask me. But if you must know, I got this when I was six years old. My dad took me to the beach that summer and yada yada…I almost drowned in the ocean. It was the worst year of my life."

Something else happened that year, but she isn't about to let go of that story.

"So, how's Seth doing?"

Her body tenses with irritation.

"Anthony, where is all of this going? This isn't what you were going to talk to me about. Come on. I haven't got any more time. I've got to get back out on the floor. Besides, you know that Seth and I are separated. We've been separated for almost six months. I don't see us getting back together. I've messed up one too many times. I've told you that. "

"That's a shame. Y'all made a cool couple and there aren't too many of those around."

As thoughtful as he sounds, she isn't sure if the appearance of sincerity is a guise.

"I always saw you two as this power couple. Loving, caring, supportive. All that stuff. The way couples are supposed to be. Like no matter what, y'all would stick by each other. It's just not right. Why the break up?"

She stands to leave.

"I'm not going to answer that. We're not the poster couple for all married couples in the world. I need to get back to work. And if you think of what you *really* were going to tell me, you know where I'll be."

He follows.

"Do you even know how good you got it?"

She faces him, ready to spit off her frustration at his line of questioning, but his panicked look stops her in her tracks.

"What's going on?"

"You know how selfish you are?"

"Where is all of this coming from? Now, I'm selfish?"

"I never had a relationship that someone loved me like Seth loves you."

Suddenly, she feels ashamed. Before she can respond, he says, "I'm in big trouble. Like, I might get arrested."

She doesn't need to ask why. It must be related to his drug dealing.

"Why do you think you're in trouble?"

"I heard through some dude in the neighborhood some detectives been asking questions about me. It doesn't look good."

While scared at the thought of being dragged into the investigation, she is mortified that her easy stream of pills will stop.

She gulps back her fears and feigning confidence, says, "I'm sure you have nothing to worry about. It's probably gossip. You know how gossip spreads like wildfire. Don't worry about it."

And there it is. She *is* an addict. And worse still, a confirmed coward. She should have encouraged him to stop his business and back it up with her addiction admission. She could have told him they could get clean and pray about it. Pray. Such a small word for a large action. They could get help together. She could have taken the role of the Christian that she professes to be. He's looking at her for answers. Instead, she chickens out, and says, "I gotta go," and leaves him looking helpless.

Chapter 5
~Charlie~

"So what did he say again?" Poppy asks as Charlie backs out of the parking spot of the assisted living facility where he has called home since his last back surgery.

"He wants to get married."

"And this is a bad thing?"

Exasperated from trying to explain a few minutes ago, she says, "It is. Because I don't want to get married. Why can't I just have a nice relationship with someone and not want to get married?"

"Because you don't want to grow old alone. And I should know. I'm an old fart and I'm alone. Besides, you already didn't give me any great-grandchildren. At least let me die knowing you've found someone to take care of you. Life's short—you better do something before it's too late. You'll be deemed an old maid soon."

"Oh gee, thanks. I don't think that term is used anymore. Besides, you had opportunities to get remarried and you never did. Why didn't you?"

Poppy pushes his glasses up, studying her with his watery blue eyes.

"I never found anyone like your grandma. You would have loved her. You are just like her, you know. Once you have the best, no one else will do. But now I'm old and alone. I guess I could have remarried and settled for a companion at least to keep me warm at night."

"Well, that's what my dog Jake is for!"

They laugh until Poppy says, "Did I ever tell you what I loved most about My Dear? You know I always called your grandmother that. Did I tell you why I called her that? When I was in Seoul, Korea… you know I fought in the Korean War, right?"

She nods like so many times before when he asks the same questions or tells the same stories or rambles on and on. "Yes, Poppy, I remember."

"Well, I would write her letters, before the days when people got lazy because of e-mail and these newfangled gadgets. Anyway, I wrote her letters all the time. And I had the worst handwriting. It was all gobbledygook. I couldn't even read my own handwriting! I always called her 'C' which was short for Catherine. One time I mucked up my greeting to her and tried to fix it on the paper I tried to write 'Dear C' but when she got my letter she thought I said *My Dear*. How she thought I wrote *My Dear*, I will never know! I didn't have the heart to tell her at that time I was just a buffoon who couldn't write and tried to fix it. By the time I did tell her I was already addressing all of the letters I wrote to her with *My Dear*. It stuck like glue. My Dear!"

Poppy chuckles softly.

And then he switches channels. "I want to talk to you about something. I want to visit my friend Marvin in Virginia before I kick the bucket."

"You need to stop talking like that. You'll outlive me."

His eyes grow wide. "I don't want to outlive you. You think I want to be George Burns or something? I've lived a good life, Charlie. I'm ready to go."

She swallows hard.

"Well, Poppy, I'm not ready. And certainly not right now. You were going to tell me the best thing about My Dear. Remember?"

He nods as he takes out his hanky and wipes his nose.

"Well, the best thing about My Dear was how she made me feel so special."

She smiles, waiting for him to continue.

"My Dear had a way to make wrong things right. She brightened my days. And she was the only one that could tell me I was a jackass and get away with it. Of course she was too much of a godly woman to say that word, but you know what I mean. She was as good as gold. That's why I'll never understand about your mother."

I drive in silence thinking about my mother. We never speak of her. She is a faded memory to me.

"I think that's a good idea to see Marvin. It's been a long time, huh?"

"I can't even remember when I saw him last. But you know about me and flying. You know I don't like to fly."

"Do you want me to fly with you?"

"Yes. I know you're busy, though. I don't want to be a burden. Does this fella like to fly?"

When Poppy asks the question, she fights the urge to remind him that he's met Lawrence twice, but instead she says, "His name is Lawrence. And you aren't a burden."

"So does this Lawrence like to fly?"

She looks at him suspiciously. "I'm not flying anywhere with Lawrence. Let's talk about you. When do you want to go?"

Poppy gazes out the window.

"Go where?"

His memory is a delicate subject.

"To Virginia. When do you want to go? I'll need to go on a weekend that I have off from work."

"Virginia? Oh… oh, as soon as possible. So let's talk about this fella again. What does he do?"

Charlie sighs.

"Poppy, I told you he's a police detective. Remember?"

"Oh, that's right. Police detective. That's a fine job. I'm sure he'll make a fine husband."

Dr. Shepherd's office is only one more street away and it's not soon enough. Sometimes it's just too painful to face the reality that his mind is going places without him.

***

As they sit in the waiting room, she flips aimlessly through magazines and wishes she could stop time and return to a season when he remembers and she doesn't feel so drained.

"Moe Schramm?" a brunette nurse calls in the waiting room.

Charlie nudges him lightly.

"Huh?"

"They're calling you. Do you want me to come with you?"

"I'm not going anywhere. What are we doing?"

Tenderly she says, "Poppy, we're at your doctor's appointment. You need to go with this nice nurse, okay?"

After the nurse helps him from the chair, Charlie walks behind him, hooking her finger around the belt loop on the back of his pants. Twice he had fallen months ago, and after refusing to use a cane, they had compromised with the belt loop. Win-win for both of them.

The nurse looks Charlie up and down.

"We'll need him to give a urine sample and get undressed, so I can come back and get you when he's done."

"Okay. Poppy, I'll see you in a few minutes."

A lump lodges in her throat as Poppy shuffles to one of the exam rooms. To relieve her mind of his illness, she reaches for her cell phone and sees where she has several text messages from the Center. After reading through those, she clicks on her Facebook account. There's a message from Andrea.

Andrea Fowler

August 21, 2012 8:42am
I was wondering whether you would be interested in sharing phone numbers. I think it might be nice to talk on the phone if you feel up to it.

What could it hurt?

She taps in her phone number, closes out her account and looks up flights to Virginia. She's barely confirmed two tickets for the weekend when she hears a commotion in one of the exam rooms. Poppy's frantic voice resounds down the hall.

Rounding the corner near the bathroom, she slips. As she catches herself, she notices the cup on the floor.

"I dropped it. I told that woman my hands were shaky. I dropped it!"

"Poppy, it's okay. It's going to be fine. No one is upset. They will clean it up."

"I'm not a child, you know. They're looking at me like I'm a child."

"No one thinks you're like a child."

"Yes, they do. I can see it in their eyes. Do they know that I served twenty years in the Marine Corps? *Semper Fi!* Do they know I fought in the Korean War? They think I can't take care of myself. You think it too, I can tell."

Her heart feels like a heavy rock. With as much courage as she can muster, she says, "It could have happened to anyone. They are used to things happening like this."

They sit quietly in the exam room. The fragments of sleepless nights stacked on top of the work exhaustion and Lawrence don't even compare to the burden she feels from Poppy's despair. She can't imagine not taking care of him, but sometimes it's more than she can bear. They are the only family each has. Her mother abandoned her so long ago that she can't remember what she looks like. There is one memory that paints a not-so-pretty picture of her, but she hangs on to it for fear that if she lets it go she won't have any memory of her at all.

***

1972

She was ready to start first grade when her mother said she would sign her up for dance lessons. When they arrived at the studio, Charlie was so petrified she squeezed her eyes shut hoping to wish her way home like Dorothy in the Wizard of Oz.

It was a scorching summer day, and her mother's grip seemed tighter than usual. She pulled Charlie to the glass counter opposite a doorway to a large room lined with mirrors. As the mirror reflected their image, Charlie saw how out of place they were—a twenty-something disheveled, unhappy woman holding the hand of a terrified brown-haired little girl.

At the counter a cheery woman greeted them and pointed to the schedule hanging on the wall. Charlie immediately liked the woman's smile. And freckles. Which were very much like her own.

She leaned across the counter as she said, "Aren't you cute. What's your name?"

The grasp tightened around her hand.

"Charlie."

"Charlie? Oh, how adorable. I don't know any girls named Charlie, but I love that name. It reminds me of 'Charlie and the Chocolate Factory.' My children love that movie. Have you ever seen it?"

Charlie nodded.

"Well, Charlie, I'm Mrs. Fishkin and this is my dance studio. I think you'll love it here once you meet all of the girls. My daughter is around here somewhere."

She pointed inside the mirror room. A bunch of girls in pink, black, and white leotards and tights were lined up on either side of the room. Most of them were holding on to the ballet bars in various poses. Even lost in her wonderment, Charlie could hear her mother's sharp tone.

"I didn't say I was signing her up. I have a good mind to leave right now, with her manners. That's not the way I taught her."

Mrs. Fishkin seemed to choose her next words carefully. "You know Mrs... I'm sorry, I don't know your name."

"Linda."

"Linda, we have a monthly special for beginner dance classes. The first two weeks are free. Do you think that might be something you want to try out for your daughter?"

Her mother released her grasp and looked down at Charlie as she asked, "What nights?"

"Tuesdays and Thursdays from seven to eight-thirty. I can sign you up tonight and she can start tomorrow night. You would just need to pay for the second two weeks."

Her mother unzipped her purse as Charlie stared at Mrs. Fishkin. Mrs. Fishkin winked in return as her mother said, "Here—sign her up. This will get her off my hands a few hours a week."

After filling out the forms, her mother grabbed her hand and headed out the door, back into the swelter. Charlie couldn't stop smiling.

Chapter 6
~Andrea~

"Mom, I folded those already."

The comment from Rochelle is followed by rolling eyes. Andrea doesn't miss a beat as she refolds the clothing making a point to do it slowly, emphasizing each fold.

"But you didn't do it like I've taught you, Rochelle. It's not worth doing if you don't do it right the first time. Especially when someone has to come behind you and fix it."

"Like seriously, Mom?"

Rochelle shakes her head at Reese, who is eating her dessert in the dining room, apparently to avoid the cross-hairs.

"It's like many things that you do—careless."

With perfect timing, Chris walks in the room and sensing the tension cautiously asks, "What's going on?"

"Mom is being difficult. She's the clothing gestapo."

"Rochelle, don't talk about your mother like that."

"She's always criticizing me!"

Unable to contain herself, Andrea stops folding.

"Really, Rochelle? I give you advice on how to do something so you can do it correctly and I am criticizing you? I'm your mother. It's my job to teach you."

"Not everyone is *perfect* like you are!" Rochelle says snidely, "You're just being unreasonable!"

"Believe me, you haven't seen unreasonable yet."

Rochelle is quiet for a few seconds and replies with, "Can I go to my room?"

Andrea takes a long look at her young, beautiful daughter, and wonders what happened to the little girl who used to sit in her lap and snuggle with her.

"Don't bother, I'll make this easy."

Aware all eyes are on her, Andrea climbs the stairs angrily to their bedroom. For good measure, she slams the door. She leans on it, wondering how things have gotten so volatile. More often than not, she and Rochelle can't even be in the same room with each other without an argument erupting. And these are the times when she sees this younger version of herself. Stubborn. Controlling. Angry.

She grabs her laptop and opens it to her conversations with Marcie and Charlie. Both have left their numbers. She mulls over whether to call one of them but can't decide which.

She and Marcie had similar personalities, which made them closer much of the time. They were more outgoing than Charlie and would come up with elaborate schemes and pranks. They also had the same sense of humor, although Marcie was the true natural when it came to it. She would do simple things like raise one side of her lip or flare her nostrils and they all would be in stitches. She would stick straws in her ears and say she was a Martian. Anyone else might have looked pathetic but Marcie made it comedic.

Andrea decides to call Marcie.

As the phone rings, she thinks about their bond. As close as they were though, they could also be like oil and vinegar. And that's when Charlie would have to referee. They were like two countries in conflict and Charlie was the United Nations. Charlie would somehow always manage to maintain peace when she was around.

Her heart drops to her stomach when she hears Marcie on the line but then realizes it's only Marcie's voicemail message.

"Hi, this is Marcie's cell phone and I'm taking messages for Marcie. Leave your message at the tone and I'll tell her when I feel like it. Just kidding. Leave your message and I'll call you back!" The voice message is followed by Marcie's laughter.

At the beep, Andrea says, "Hello, Marcie. You haven't changed a bit according to your message! Ever since we found each other online I've been doing a lot of reminiscing. We have a lot to share and I'm really looking forward to it. Call me when you have a moment and we can play catch up. Look forward to talking to you soon."

***

1972

The Fishkin back yard was known to harbor more than just the average child's play equipment and toys. It had a myriad of other treasures that the neighborhood children knew about and wanted to see. And what most parents in the neighborhood looked at as a junkyard, children viewed as an amusement park. It was well known for miles around and so was Andrea's eccentric mother who had collected most of it.

In the spring of third grade, she invited Marcie and Charlie to play one Saturday afternoon. A few of the neighborhood kids also came over, including her former enemy turned friend, Christopher.

Playtime started innocently enough with everyone climbing the backyard trees, swinging on the swing-set, throwing balls, and playing freeze tag. But then, to Andrea's disapproval, Marcie came up with an idea to play out the scene of a Three Stooges circus episode for the neighborhood kids.

"We've already done that before. Nobody wants to do that. We need to build a fort!"

"We did that last time," Marcie insisted. "Besides, this time we can do the tightrope walker part."

"Charlie, you don't want to do that, do you?"

"I want to do that," Christopher piped in.

Andrea gave the evil eye to Christopher who instantly stepped back. Charlie said diplomatically, "Maybe we should ask what everyone wants to do."

Andrea rolled her eyes. "Okay, who wants to do what I said?"

To her great disappointment, not one hand raised. Charlie shrugged her shoulders. Defeated, Andrea walked away from the group of kids who seemed eager to follow her friend. She sat on her favorite tire swing, with her back to them.

"What are you doing?"

It was Charlie.

"I don't want to play with you babies anyway."

"Please play, Andrea. It won't be the same without you."

Christopher stood behind Charlie grinning. It was hard to say no.

The Three Stooges Circus became a huge hit. The three used every item in the yard to entertain their crowd. But the hit was the tightrope act. They used every ounce of talent they had as they displayed courage and strength. It was also a turning point in the relationship as they became steadfast friends.

Chapter 7
~Marcie~

*F*or the millionth time, Marcie looks at the dashboard, lead foot on the pedal, determined not to be late for work again. This time Kesha might not listen to another excuse. She's certain she's overstepped her quotas.

Seth's text messages are to blame. They built up in her inbox until she finally opened one to see his message on reconciling. She's not ready to talk yet. And the conversation with Anthony the day before still has her rattled.

She rushes into the gym almost knocking Kesha over.

"Marcie, are you okay?"

"I'm so sorry, Kesha."

"Don't worry about it." And then she turns serious. "I'm glad you ran into me. We need to talk. Get your stuff settled and come to my office in five minutes."

Panic sets in. She's been found out.

"Gotcha." Her attempt at being calm may have come across as too nonchalant She kicks herself mentally.

Seconds seem like minutes and the five minutes seem like an hour as she contemplates how she will respond to Kesha's accusations. She will definitely have to reason with her. Begging is not out of the question.

First, she hits the locker room. After splashing water on her face she says to the mirror, *"Come clean to her. Tell her what's been going on."* As if preparing for the fight of her life, she grabs a paper towel, dries her face and heads to Kesha's office. Kesha wastes no time.

"Something has been brought to my attention and I hate that I have to address this with you."

Marcie puts on her best poker face, deciding, at least for this moment, she will play politician and deny vehemently any charges against her.

"How long have we known each other?" Kesha asks.

"I don't know—ten years? It was right after I stopped teaching and that was ten years ago. Why?"

"I just feel like we have a good friendship and what I am about to tell you is difficult."

Marcie squirms in her seat. *Here it comes!*

Kesha says, "I found out something yesterday that was quite disturbing."

"What?"

Just say it.

"I can't believe that this was happening right under my nose. I thought that we all had such honest relationships."

Not being able to hold her tongue any long, Marcie says, "There is something I should—"

"It's Anthony," Kesha interrupts. "You're friends with him, aren't you?"

"Sort of. We knew each other from the high school we worked at."

"I am telling you this because of your friendship with him and I can trust your discretion. Anthony got caught yesterday in a drug sting. Narcotics. Mostly hydrocodone and oxycontin. Apparently it's something that he's been part of for the last couple of years."

Marcie waits for the other shoe to drop.

"He called me from jail last night. He doesn't have any family that's in the area and he wanted my help."

"Wow. I can't believe it."

"I just can't help but wonder how much of this has trickled down to the clients at the gym—or even the staff. Do you think that he was selling to anyone here or providing anything else, like steroids?"

And here comes the other shoe.

"I don't think so." The lie catches in her throat like dry crackers.

"Do you ever remember seeing anything suspicious?

Anything that made you wonder? I really trust your honesty, Marcie."

"Well, there is something that I should tell you—" The phone rings and breaks her thought.

"Hold on. Hello? Yes. Just a moment."

Kesha looks up and says, "Let's continue this later. I've got to answer this call, okay? Thank you for coming in and talking to me. And please, this is confidential. Don't talk to anyone about what I've told you."

"Sure. We'll talk later."

As Marcie stands, her legs feel like rubber. She barely makes it out of the office, aware her heart feels as if it will beat out of her chest. She quickly assesses the need for something to hold her together. She's in such a daze she doesn't notice the small figure trying to get her attention.

"Marcie?" A hand waves in front of her. It's Edith Macklin from Good Tidings Church.

Perhaps she doesn't look as frazzled as she feels, but she doubts it. She puts on her best perky face.

"Mrs. Macklin, how are you today? You're looking mighty sporty there! I thought you were one of our fitness gurus! "

Mrs. Macklin giggles and says earnestly, "I'm doing okay, Marcie. My rheumatoid is acting up severely today so I don't think that I'm going to be able to do my usual routine. Plus I don't see that young man who usually helps me. Tony, is it?"

"Are you talking about Anthony?"

Marcie imagines telling Mrs. Macklin about Anthony's predicament. Word would be spread around the gym in less than five minutes. Telephone... Telegraph... Tell Mrs. Macklin. She takes the safe road, and tells a white lie. They seem to be flowing off her tongue like King Midas's gold.

"Anthony's out sick today."

"Oh, that's a shame. Such a good young man. He's always so helpful. Well, pass the word to him that I was asking for him and I will say a prayer for his healing. Pastor Sinclair was just preaching the other day about healing. What did he say? Let me see... it was in Isaiah 53. By his stripes we are healed! You know that one, right? Are you going to church tonight? I haven't seen you lately."

Mrs. Macklin is right. She doesn't want to be seen. And especially at church. On Sunday when she tiptoed in late and listened to the healing sermon by Pastor Sinclair she felt so unworthy, she snuck out the back, certain no one saw her. But what could she say now? She doesn't have any reason not to go. Besides, she already told one lie to Mrs. Macklin about Anthony. She couldn't tell another to the sweet old lady.

"I'll be there tonight."

And then for good measure she says, "Why don't you save me a seat?"

***

Driving home she can't rid herself of the pins and needles from the day. Seth's badgering. Kesha's news about Anthony. Mrs. Macklin's expectations. The constant knee pain. And the last pill she took didn't even make a mark on the throbbing in her body.

The guilt of the past year is eating her alive. She's sure it's the cause of her frequent bouts of heart palpitations and dizziness. Passing out is inevitable. With only a few pills left and no chance of getting any filled soon, she decides to try a different route of relief.

With Anthony out of commission, she must conserve what pills she has. But there is still the dilemma of sleep. She makes a detour on the way home and stops at the drugstore.

She knows where the sleeping medication is and takes little time searching it out and grabbing a bottle. She heads toward the front counter, but stops short at the blood pressure machine.

Once her arm is in the cuff, she presses the start button and waits. Within a minute, the results flash on the display—one hundred fifty over ninety-seven. Not a good sign.

She starts her trek again to the storefront, this time caught off guard by two people standing at the pharmacist's counter—an elderly woman holding the hand of a little girl who looks about eight years old. There is something very familiar about the girl.

Trying not to get caught staring, she walks by them and hears the girl ask, "Grandma, can we get ice cream on our way home?" She recognizes the voice. Sophia.

Sophia, the girl they had fostered for six months, is playing with her hair, seemingly oblivious to anything that isn't related to an ice cream cone. In Marcie's current state of mind she knows she can't talk to her. It will be too painful. She struggles with the urge, pays for the sleeping pills, and rushes to her car for refuge.

It is there that the dam breaks and the bottled-up tears finally flow. The months the three of them had as a happy family flash in her mind. Seth, Sophia, and Marcie. They were the three Musketeers. Seth loved her as much as Marcie did. Those were the happiest moments of her life.

In between teardrops, she manages a smile thinking about happier times with Sophia. Seth would be the bucking bronco to Sophia's cowgirl, which remind her of her father and the fun times she had with him.

By the time she gets home, the images of Seth are resonating along with those of her father when she was a little girl. It's too much to think about and the tears come faster.

Although it's early, she skips dinner, settles into her bed and pops two sleeping pills. Right before she drifts to sleep she remembers her promise to Mrs. Macklin to come to church. It is yet another reminder of the promises she fails to keep.

Chapter 8
~Charlie~

*T*he final notes of her report on the Taylor family lay on the table in front of her. Domestic violence. Alcoholism. Children with special needs. A typical case file. And as usual another sleepless night.

Charlie heats up canned spaghetti and gobbles it up between reading over her painstaking notes about the family. Between the sleeplessness and stress, she's worked up another appetite.

She has to impress her boss, Mr. Jimenez, since he approved the time off for her trip. But he made it very clear that her closeout reports must be completed before she left.

At one point, in between the keys clacking and fork shoveling, her cell phone buzzes with a text message. Only one person would think of texting so late.

Hope I'm not waking u. I figure u would be working hard at ur computer.

She flushes at Lawrence's accurate assumption. He knows her well.

Yep. Finishing up work.

Seconds later, another text.

Thought about what u said & want to apologize for pushing u into something ur not ready for. U should have the best in life & sometimes I don't think u believe that. I shouldn't have left so abruptly but I wasn't prepared for what u said. I assumed u felt the same as me.

Charlie lets the words sink in. He apologizes to her! She broke his heart and he apologizes to her. Now besides being the worst girlfriend, she's the worst friend in the world.

As if playing chess, she contemplates his next move. If she chooses to text him back, he might call and she isn't ready for a conversation with him. She might say something that she didn't mean or, worse yet, might say something she did mean. She settles on texting.

I'm sorry too. I've got to go. I'll talk to you tomorrow.

Sweet and to the point. She places the phone down and realizes she needs to tell Marcie and Andrea something.

Charlie Baldwin
Thursday, August 23, 2012 1:42 am
Marcie & Andrea – Wanted to let you know I'll be in town this weekend. My grandpa (Remember Poppy?) wants to visit friends so I'm flying up with him on Friday. I know this is kind of last minute, but do you think you both could spare a couple of hours? Maybe we

could meet for dinner? It's been such a long time since I've been there, so you will need to pick the place. Let me know if that's something that you can do. I really would love to see both of you.

She reads it over before clicking send. Looking at the piles of reports, she remembers Mr. Jimenez's words of caution about getting all the work done.

A familiar clicking approaches. Jake sits, staring at her. His favorite stuffed animal is trapped between his jaws. It tickles her. The poor toy is so worn it barely has any fur on it and yet Jake clings to it as if it's his best friend. She takes it gently and tosses it, to which he responds immediately by retrieving it in a matter of seconds. So easy to please. So easy to care for. He expects so little—a little food, a little playing time, and a little attention. Nothing too complicated; he's easy to figure out.

If only things were that easy with Lawrence. He requires so much more. Not that he's demanding. He never demands anything of her but his needs are much more complicated. She doesn't want to let him down. And what if one day he finally sees the age difference and says, "Who is this old lady?"

She turns her attention to the rabbit again. It reminds her of an old stuffed animal she had years ago.

***

1972

At the risk of getting spanked, she turned on the television to drown out the dead quiet of the apartment. She sat holding her favorite kangaroo, Kangy, which had bald spots from weeks of pulling out the fur. Sucking her index finger helped, but she was starting to get a sore from it. Besides, she hated when her mother called her a baby.

It felt like a long time since she was dropped off. As her mother left the apartment she yelled, "I'll be right back. I'm just going to get some cigarettes. Don't open the door to no one," and then the door slammed.

The television provided a little comfort. She watched "All in the Family" and smiled when the laughter came on even though she had no idea what they were laughing about. The funny old man with the cigar reminded her of Poppy, which made her feel better.

The phone rang and she ran through the cluttered floor to her mother's bedroom door. It was locked. She had started locking the door recently and Charlie was told never to enter.

Not able to get to the phone, she returned to the living room. The phone rang over and over and then finally stopped.

At some time during the news hour, her stomach growled and she got up to see what she could find to eat in the kitchen. Leftover tomato soup, a rotten apple, and a bottle of juice. She grabbed the juice and poured it into a plastic cup, accidently spilling some on the counter. She wiped it quickly, knowing she would be yelled at for that. When she was done, she snuck two Oreos from the package on the counter, grabbed her juice and returned to the living room. She placed the food on the floor and sat next to it.

Moses, her calico, rubbed up against her. She pulled him to her lap and patted his soft head, making him purr. After kissing him, she let him go. He sniffed at her cookies. He was hungry too. He finally walked away meowing.

The phone rang again. Familiar loneliness came over Charlie. Her mother had left her many times before. She always hated it. She would rather be treated poorly than be left alone. The phone finally stopped ringing.

She sang her favorite song that Poppy taught her shortly after Moses came along:

"Oh Señor Don Gato was a cat, Meow.
On a high red roof Don Gato sat. Meow.
He went there to read a letter, Meow, meow, meow."

Moses, who had given up trying to find something to eat, trotted over.

"Where the reading light was better,
'Twas a love note for Don Gato."

She pushed up from the floor and danced around in a circle, hands raised. Forgetting some of the song, she fumbled with the words and hopped at the beat of every "meow."

"La la la... jumped so merrily, Meow
He fell off the roof and broke his knee. Ow!
Broke his ribs and all his whiskers, Meow, meow, meow."

Moses chased her until she picked him up.

"Aye caramba!!! cried poor Don Gato"

As he hung from her arms, she didn't think Moses liked her singing.

"But even though they tried, Meow
Poor Señor Don Gato up and died. Meow
Oh it wasn't very merry, Meow, meow, meow
Going to the cemetery, Meow, meow, meow
For the end of poor Don Gato!"

And with the last word of the song, she landed on the floor with a large thump causing Moses to drop from her arms and dart frantically around the room.

Charlie was catching her breath, when she heard a knock. She ran to the front door and eagerly unlocked it. It had to be her mother.

But it wasn't. It was Poppy. He stood with empty bags in his hand, sweat pouring from his brow. She was delighted.

"Poppy! What are you doing here?"

Charlie hugged his belly.

"I came by to see you and your mom. Are you supposed to open this door without asking who's behind it? Where's your mom? I tried calling. Why didn't anyone answer? Are you by yourself?"

His face was red. As he entered the apartment, she said, "She went to get something to eat."

Did he know she was lying?

He shook his head and gritted his teeth as he looked around the room. The apartment was in disarray and filthy. The stench of cigarette smoke and mildew wafted through the air and he immediately ordered, "Get your stuff… I'm getting you out of this hole."

Charlie couldn't move. She'd never seen him so angry. He took notice and said softly, "I'm not angry at you. I just want you to be safe. And a six-year-old does not belong in an apartment alone. So I just want you to come home with me for a bit. Gather your clothes. You can bring Moses."

She loved Poppy more than any other person in the world. Even more than she loved her mother. And she trusted him. Happy to comply, she immediately went to her room and yanked clothes out of her closet and drawers. Poppy followed and began tossing the clothes into the brown paper sacks.

She picked up her cat as they made their way to the front door. When they reached it, she handed him to Poppy.

"I forgot something."

She ran back and snatched up Kangy, still on the floor in front of the television. She looked at the apartment one final time, glad to escape it.

Chapter 9
~Andrea~

Wednesday's argument is still fresh in Andrea's mind Thursday morning. She feels daggers from both daughters as she prepares breakfast.

The mood at the kitchen table is somber. Rochelle, has decided to eat cereal and is finishing the last of her bowl. Silence is her armor. Andrea glances periodically at the miniature version of herself.

Reese finally breaks the uncomfortable quiet and says, "You need help?"

"Please. Just grab some plates so I can put these omelets on them."

As Reese helps, Chris walks cautiously into the kitchen.

"Charlie and Marcie coming this weekend?"

Andrea nods.

After everyone has their food, she sits at her usual seat and says, "I asked them to come over this Saturday for brunch." She doesn't bother giving any details she is sure will bore them. They have no idea the painstaking time and energy it takes to keep a house running and put together meals.

Rochelle stands and addresses Chris.

"May I be excused? I'm going to be late."

"Yes. Whose turn is it to help with the dishes?"

Andrea waves them off. "I'll handle it. Reese is taking you to school, right?"

When Rochelle finally finishes and exits, the tension in the room is thick as molasses. Reese gobbles up the last of hers and follows Rochelle's lead, leaving Chris and Andrea alone.

He clears his throat. "Andrea, I think that we need to discuss—"

"I don't have time to discuss anything right now. I have a lot to do."

"You keep saying that but I think that we need to prioritize our family's happiness."

"*Happiness?* What do you mean *prioritize* our family's happiness? Every day I prioritize everyone's happiness. Remember, I'm the one cooking and cleaning and making sure all of the daily things are done to make sure that this family runs smoothly. As well as putting bacon on the table."

"You know that's not what I'm talking about."

"What are you talking about, Chris?"

He rubs his temple. Andrea goes in for the kill.

"As usual, when it comes to really saying anything important you clam up! Besides, *All Fed Up* is calling me today to tell me what they think about my work. I really need this job."

As he hangs his head, he says, "We can't keep going on like this. You need help. We need help."

Help? Who is he to say that she needs help? He can't even keep his household straight.

She stops short of throwing more barbs at him. She doesn't have the time. In a lower tone, she says, "We can talk later, okay?" To show her good intentions she touches his shoulder. "Really—"

He pulls away.

"What do you think I am? A doormat? You don't think that I'm also affected in all of this? As always, it's the world according to Andrea. Whatever Andrea wants, whatever Andrea says!"

Startled, she steps back. Chris never reacts with such anger. Stewing, she watches him gather his tablet and keys, skipping his usual goodbye routine, and leaves the house with an, "I'll see you later."

The girls hurry out a few minutes later, leaving her with the dishes and the morning's quarrel unsettled. Avoiding the obvious problems of their household, she puts her thoughts into the reunion with Marcie and Charlie. She envisions preparing a delicious meal and showing off her house and begins to feel better. So much that she calls Charlie. The phone rings once.

"Hello?"

"Charlie?"

"Yes?"

"Charlie, this is Andrea Fishkin Fowler."

Andrea feels uneasy. Does she sound too eager? What if Charlie doesn't have time for her? What will she say? It's always easier to hide behind keystrokes.

"Hi, Andrea! I was hoping that you would call. How are you?"

Andrea is relieved.

"I'm great. How in the world are you?"

"Things are going well. I'm looking forward to seeing you this weekend. Our flight gets in at eight-thirty tomorrow night and then I'm going to take the rental car to the hotel. Poor Poppy hates flying. You remember him, right?"

"I do. I remember him bringing you to the dance studio and over to my house."

"Oh, I remember that too. We have so much to catch up on! Anyway, because he hates flying, I'm a little skeptical of planning anything that night. And he will be mostly spending time with Marvin. But I'm really looking forward to coming over Saturday."

"Well, I've got brunch covered for us and will see you at eleven. I'll forward you the directions to the house."

"Brunch sounds really good. So I'll see you then."

As she hangs up, Andrea grabs a notepad and pen and puts together her grocery list, almost forgetting her meeting. Their talk has her thinking about more than just the dance studio.

***

1972

She looked past the desk and plants until they focused on the parking lot of Jefferson Elementary. Her mother should have been there already, she was sure of it. She panned to the principle, Mrs. Stokes, and back to the lot in time to see the familiar green station wagon. Her mother was searching for a spot.

Licking her lip, which was already cracked from one too many licks, Andrea prepared herself for what was to come.

She wasn't afraid of punishment from her mother as it would most likely include something at the dance studio or maybe sorting her ugly buttons. That didn't scare her. It was how her mother would act that worried Andrea. Even at her young age, she recognized that her mother was very different from other adults she met.

This wasn't the first time she was sent to the principal's office but this was the first time she caused this much trouble. *What would her mother say this time?*

Her mother pulled into a spot, and looked at herself in the rear-view mirror. From such a long distance, it was impossible to see the features on her face, but Andrea pictured the dark circles under her eyes she noticed that morning. They made her look like a raccoon.

Through the other school incidents involving Andrea the previous year, her mother had gotten to know the principal, Gloria Stokes, and established a relationship with her. It turned out that Mrs. Stokes was Marcie's mother.

"Are you listening, Andrea?"

She was caught.

"Yes Ma'am."

Mrs. Stokes motioned for Andrea and Christopher to get up. They both followed obediently and when she pointed to the chairs in the administration area, Andrea eagerly sat. She didn't want to make things worse.

When her mother walked in, Andrea raised her hand and waved, as if she had just won a contest and not given a boy a black eye and wreaked havoc on an otherwise normal recess hour. She gave her a *what-did-you-do-now* look and followed Mrs. Stokes.

The door shut.

Andrea's chicken legs swung nervously. Christopher, who was still holding a bag of ice on his cheek, asked, "Are you gonna be in a lot of trouble?"

She cocked her head. What did he care?

"Naw. You?"

"Yeah. My dad said to never fight. Especially with a girl."

She suddenly felt sorry for him.

Soon she could hear her mother say to Mrs. Stokes, "So good to see you. Of course, not under these circumstances, though."

"Yes, it seems that Andrea had quite the morning. Andrea decided it was okay to beat up Christopher Fowler this morning and her actions caused quite a mess on the playground. Not that this makes it right—but Christopher wasn't innocent in this. He apparently was leading his friends in teasing her and from the looks of it he pulled her hair as well. His father will be here shortly."

"So, you could call this self-defense?"

"Not exactly. She hurt Christopher so much he has a nice shiner."

"You know how strong-willed she is. I swear I don't know where she gets it from. Michael calls her our *Kemfer*. That's a Yiddish word for fighter. Having three brothers has toughened her up. You know, she has never been one to play with dolls and dress up. She wants to play with her brothers' Rock'Em Sock'Em robots or throw the football with them."

"Yes, but, Mrs. Fishkin, they aren't the ones in here, she is. Andrea has so much potential, you know. Her teacher is amazed at how well she reads and can already multiply her numbers. I hate to see such God-given talent wasted."

There was a long pause before her mother said, "I agree. I just think if we could focus her energy on something else…do you have any suggestions?"

"I'm glad you asked. I want you to think about her helping my daughter, Marcie. Has she met her yet?"

"I think one of the times when Andrea came with me to the studio. You think she would be able to do that? What does she need help with?"

"Well, you heard about the beach incident I'm sure. Ever since then Marcie has had a hard time concentrating. I thought I could help her through this but Marcie is really struggling with simple math problems as well as her reading. And, of course you know that my husband died so suddenly as well so she is just having such a hard time. It was such a blow to all of us."

Her eyes grew wide as she recalled the story about Marcie almost drowning in the summer. She leaned towards the door and heard her mother whisper, "I am so sorry for your loss."

"Thank you. I think that Marcie is so confused right now with adults that it might be helpful to have a child tutor her. It won't be anything difficult. Just something that Andrea could explain in the way she understands it. But you know I still need to suspend Andrea for three days. Would you be able to take her to the studio with you?"

Andrea mulled over Mrs. Stokes words. What did she mean *tutor* Marcie?

Minutes later, her mother was thanking Mrs. Stokes and left her office. Andrea trotted behind.

Nothing was said on the way to the car. She didn't like her mother's silence. It wasn't a good sign.

Finally, after they drove away from the school, her mother said, "You can't go to school for the next three days."

"Oh goody! I don't like school anyway,"

The car came to a stop.

"Don't think that you're getting off easy, young lady. This isn't going to be a fun time. I want you to really think about what you did. You could have really hurt Christopher, do you realize that?"

Her mother looked in time to see Andrea scrunch her face and stick out her tongue.

"Andrea, I'm not kidding. This has got to stop."

"But, Mommy, he deserved it! He pulled my hair and called me fish can! All of those ugly boys did. My last name's not fish can, it's Fishkin. I told them that."

And that's when her mother put her head on the steering wheel. Andrea had gone too far.

"Mommy, what's wrong?"

It seemed like forever until she finally looked up. Her raccoon eyes were darker. She was crying.

"Why can't you be a good girl? Why can't you be like other little girls?"

For once in her young life, Andrea didn't know what to say. Her mother wiped her eyes before starting up the car again.

"Well, besides the suspension, Mrs. Stokes has something else that she wants you to do. Do you remember meeting Marcie right before school ended in June? She had blond curly hair that went to her shoulders and she was really silly and funny? You seemed to like her."

"Oh, I remember her! Remember she said that knock-knock joke! Knock knock? Who's there? Banana. Banana who? Knock knock. Who's there? Banana. Banana Who? Knock knock. Who's there? Orange. Orange who? Orange you glad I didn't say banana?" and then she laughed hysterically. When her mother smiled, Andrea knew things were going to be okay. At least for the day.

***

The computer buzzes, reminding Andrea of her meeting. As the screen comes into focus, she hides her disappointment with a big smile. Instead of Maggie Ryan on the screen, it's her assistant, Callie Barton again.

"Hi, Andrea. How are you today?"

Callie doesn't have the same spark that she had during their previous chat.

"I'm doing well, Callie. I'm very excited to hear what Ms. Ryan thinks of my work."

"Well, Andrea..." Callie looks down for a second. Andrea tenses for the bad news.

"First I want to let you know that Ms. Ryan was very pleased with your work. She felt that not only was it creative but also innovative and unique. Very promising for sure."

The accolades feel good but aren't enough.

"I'm so glad she liked it. I worked very hard and I can assure you that is what I will be able to produce—and better if you allow me to work with this company. I will work however long it takes to give you all what you need."

Callie clears her throat before she says, "That's what I need to talk to you about. Do you remember I told you Ms. Ryan was sick the last time that we talked? Well, she is sicker than any of us thought and she has taken a leave of absence for a while."

Andrea takes in this new information.

"I'm sorry to hear that. Please pass on my well wishes…and prayers."

Prayers? Her prayer life had taken a siesta years ago.

"Certainly. I know that she will appreciate that. So, what I need to really tell you is this. And believe me when I say that this was a very difficult decision to make. You know we have different magazines out on the market. Well, we have decided to cut some of the projects that we are currently working. We already were experiencing some bad effects from the economy and then when this happened with Ms. Ryan, well… you can imagine. Because of that we won't be able to use all of the submissions that we've received. Yours is included in those. Please don't think that your work isn't good. We would like you to submit again perhaps next year when we get back on our feet."

As Andrea quiets the anger building up, she mumbles, "I understand. Thank you for taking the time to call me back. Again, please tell her I'm praying for her."

She almost chokes on the blasphemy spewing from her mouth. She doesn't feel thankful and she's forgotten how to pray. She watches the screen go blank.

Stewing in her disappointment, she decides to channel some of her anger into tackling the wash. She becomes so engrossed in the piles of clothes, she doesn't hear Reese come in. They almost collide in the family room.

Reese's boyfriend, Adrian, is standing next to her. He is adorned in ear gages, a tank top and shorts that show off more than a dozen tattoos. And although he claims to go to the local community college and works as a waiter at a restaurant, he doesn't seem very motivated when it comes to worldly success.

"Hey, Mom. We're just going swimming. You have any towels in your basket?"

"No, but there are some in the closet."

"I'll get us a couple. Adrian, why don't you wait outside for me? I'll be right there." In an instant, she has left Andrea and Adrian to themselves.

"Hi, Mrs. Fowler." Adrian smiles.

"I thought you were taking classes this summer."

"I am. I take them all on-line. Much easier."

That figures.

"Do you know what you want to do?"

"Not really. I'm just taking general studies. I'm thinking I might go into the military, though."

Andrea raises her eyebrows.

"Well, you have a lot of cleaning up to do, don't you think?"

"I guess so. I definitely would have to get rid of some of this stuff." He answers as he points to one of his gages.

"Adrian, why don't you go outside and I'll grab a couple of cold drinks for you two."

He nods. "Thanks."

When he's gone, Andrea lets out a long sigh.

Reese has walked back into the room just in time to hear her and says, "What's wrong, Mom? You look mad."

"What do you possibly see in him?"

"A lot. Just give him a chance." She walks to the kitchen and Andrea is on her heels.

"Reese, I'm just wondering. He just seems like he doesn't care about anything. And the military? Does he really want to go into the military? Really? The way he looks now he might be better off to be a professional tattoo display. And the hair…"

Reese grabs the glasses of lemonade and makes her way to the back door. "Mom, would you leave him alone?"

"I just think that you can do better."

"I don't think that's why you don't like him, Mom. I think that you don't like him because he's Filipino."

Andrea stops Reese at the door. "Are you accusing me of being racist? You actually think I don't like him because he's Filipino?

"Well, you didn't like Ty either, remember?"

"Reese, did you forget that Ty treated you like dirt? I didn't forget because I was there to put back the pieces of your life that he ruined!"

Reese opens the door and answers quietly, "Adrian's not like that. He's sweet and caring. You just need to give him a chance." Reese shuts the door leaving Andrea to stew some more.

Chapter 10
~Marcie~

Relishing the warmth of the covers, Marcie dreads the thought of getting up. She hasn't slept this well in months. Two sleeping pills gave her the rest of Sleeping Beauty, and like a fairy tale, she doesn't want it to end. She starts to drift back to slumber when the awful realization jolts her. Her alarm didn't go off.

Frantically she dashes around the bedroom, throwing on fitness attire and makeup like a mad woman, aware the damage is already done. This time will be different with Kesha. Her tardiness quotient has already been met. Firing is imminent.

She's barely in the car, rolling down her window, when she realizes the needle for the gas is registering one hair over empty. Seth usually takes care of that for her.

"Ugh!"

Two teenage girls passing her bumper look at her in surprise.

"That wasn't aimed at you!" she shouts.

Her explanation is met with mocking smiles as one touches her head before they take to the sidewalk and disappear. *Was that gesture aimed at her?* She looks in the rearview mirror. Her hair looks like a bird's nest.

With a quick finger-comb through the knots, she takes to the street like a veteran race driver. Each turn faster than the last, coasting through the green lights as if they are lit brightly just for her. She nods to her invisible passenger and feels for a moment that she will make it. False alarm. She will still have her job. Until the siren blasting behind her only a mile from the gym tells her otherwise.

She could just cry. Again.

"Please get out your license and registration. Ma'am, are you aware what the speed limit is?"

The police officer rubs his cheek, most likely anticipating the fib Marcie will tell.

"I think forty."

"No, Ma'am. It's thirty. And are you aware the speed that you were going?"

"I'm not sure."

"You were going fifty."

Marcie swallows, certain the tears will flow as she pictures not only being jobless, but also homeless after her insurance goes through the roof. A few months back she received a ticket for going through a red light. A month before that she caused a car accident. Seth really reamed her for that one since it was his car. It never drove the same after that.

The officer hands her the speeding ticket offering advice on slowing down and staying out of trouble. She nods and tosses the ticket in her cup holder before easing into traffic.

Once she arrives at the gym, she hobbles through the parking lot, thinking about her plight and is met by Kesha at the door. This time there is no friendly morning greeting, no fond smile, and no willingness in her eyes to forgive the tardiness.

"Don't bother going into the locker room. Let's talk in my office," Kesha says coldly.

As they sit, Marcie feels the familiarity of the day before. But unlike that conclusion, this will be different. Kesha struggles with her words.

"Marcie, I need to ask you something but I want to see if you have something that you want to tell me first. Has everything been all right with you lately? I know you have some things going on in your personal life and I don't want to pry, but I want you to know that if you need to talk to someone about them I am here for you."

"Thank you."

She continues, "I know that this year has been hard with your knees and unfortunately in our line of work, it has made it very difficult for you. By the way, how are they feeling today?"

Just tell her everything. You might not get another chance. But even the reassuring look doesn't persuade her.

"Everything is doing much better. Thanks."

The look of disappointment on Kesha's face is evident. And even more so as she asks, "How are things with Seth?"

"Fine," Marcie answers, more quickly than she planned.

Kesha sighs and says, "I can't force you to talk to me or tell me anything but I'm going to put you on a leave of absence for a few days. I can't allow you to be late to work anymore. And some of the customers are complaining that you aren't taking the time with them as you should. I already warned you about that as well. I think you would agree that I have been more than lenient when it comes to your tardiness. You have some leave you haven't taken so I want you to take it today and Monday. And then I want you to call me on Tuesday. I'll let you know at that time if you need to come in."

Kesha takes out a stack of business cards in her desk drawer and hands one to Marcie. "You may want to call this number if you need any help."

Chapter 11
~Charlie~

The flickering runway lights at Norfolk International Airport represent more than guidance for the plane, they offer Charlie hope for new beginnings.

As she anticipates their arrival and the ultimate reunion with Marcie and Andrea, she rests her head against the window pane to get a better look at the illuminated city lights below. Poppy sleeps soundly next to her as the plane prepares for landing.

Putting her book away, it hits her that it truly has been too long since she visited. It wasn't done on purpose. Poppy had taken her away from the area at such a young age that Charlie really didn't feel grounded and had no reason to return but twice at Poppy's request.

"Poppy, it's time to get up. We're getting ready to land."

"It's not time yet. Just another minute," Poppy grumbles as he turns his head away.

Charlie pauses before she tries again.

"Poppy, you've got to wake up. Once we get to our hotel you can go to sleep for the night." She gently nudges his shoulder and he responds with a slap on her shoulder.

"I said it's not time yet. Reveille hasn't played yet. Leave me alone or I'm gonna hurt you."

"Poppy, it's me, Charlie."

He opens his eyes slowly and she sighs with relief until he says, "Charlie? I don't know a Charlie. Who are you?"

Sorrow sucker punches her. His memory lapses are happening more often. Treading carefully is a must so as not to upset him and cause a scene.

Poppy watches her cautiously and she decides to play it normal.

"Did you sleep well?"

"I don't think so. I didn't sleep well. Where am I? Where's My Dear? I told her I'd be home soon."

He looks around the cabin, his face full of confusion. The stewardesses is calling for trays to be folded and seats put in their upright positions. As Charlie contemplates how to handle him, he closes his eyes again. She takes the opportunity to try to fasten his seatbelt.

As she places the metal fitting into the buckle, his hand squeezes her neck. Gasping, she looks into his eyes. He clearly does not know who she is.

"What are you doing? Leave me alone. Get off of me!"

The man in the seat across the aisle has gotten out of his seat and attempts to help. He distracts Poppy enough to loosen his grip around Charlie. In disbelief, she pulls away, massaging her neck. Although his episodes had increased, he had never gotten violent.

Within moments two stewardesses, as well as another man, crowd around Poppy which only adds to his confusion.

"Stop, please. He doesn't understand. Please don't scare him. Let me try to talk to him. Please don't hurt him. He's an Alzheimer patient."

"Ma'am, we have to look out for the safety of all of our passengers."

"I understand, but wait, please." Aware of the scared passengers around her, Charlie fumbles in her purse for her wallet. She searches until she pulls out a small picture of My Dear.

"Look, Poppy. Here's a picture of My Dear. She loved you so much."

A blissful look comes over his face.

"Charlie, are we almost there?"

"We're just getting ready to land."

"Oh, good. Marvin is expecting me, you know."

***

Poppy is relaxed in the hotel bed shortly after they get their room and is sleeping once his head hits the pillow. Meanwhile, Charlie can't even think of sleep.

It's only ten-thirty and she's still wound from the flight's event, grateful the crew released them once they checked him over. Charlie knows for sure she will take him to Dr. Shepherd and see about another center that will suit him better. It will absolutely kill him to be stuck in a permanent facility. He will hate her for it.

To clear her mind, she checks her messages and sees one from Andrea.

Saturday is right around the corner! As promised here are the directions to my house. Please call me if you need help with it. See you at 11:00.

Since it's too late to call, she continues checking the messages. Most are from Mr. Jimenez, a reminder that she is not entirely on vacation.

She answers the messages quickly, making mental notes of what she needs to take care of when she returns and then she finishes looking through the rest of the messages. There is another one from Lawrence.

I guess the fact that u aren't answering my texts is my sign it's over. If it's not too much, I'd like to get my things from ur house. U available Saturday?

Is it truly over? Is she ready to move on? She can't imagine life without him.

Like Jake, he's fun, and brings warmth and comfort but is she really ready for the next step. Something is getting in her way. She just can't pinpoint what it is. And she doesn't want to cause him more pain while she figures it out. He deserves better. She texts back.

I'll still be gone on Saturday. I can call you when I return.

Instead of a response text, her phone rings. She can't talk to him. Not in her current frame of mind. She waits for it to go to voicemail, but it rings again. It's too much to listen to and she starts to change the ringer but slides the receiver instead.

"Lawrence?"

"Look, Charlie, I'm not going to keep bothering you. I'll get my things when you get back. I just wanted to know if someone is watching Jake for you."

Jake. Normally Lawrence helps out with Jake but she took him to the vet this time.

"Don't tell me you took him to a dog kennel."

"No. I took him to Dr. Pinter's office."

"Charlie…come on. Let me get him. I'll watch him until you get home. He's going to end up with Parvo or kennel cough or something."

She shakes her head at the irony. Lawrence didn't even like dogs when he met her and now he is Dr. Doolittle. He even suggests the best dog food to feed Jake and to stay away from the kind that has artificial colors and cheap fillers, and the best treats to give him so he doesn't gain too much weight.

"Okay. Can you take him to your house?"

"Sure. I'll take good care of him."

Chapter 12
~Andrea~

Just breathe. Deep breaths to calm your nerves.

Andrea paces the dining room, eyeing the spread laid out for brunch. Enough food for an army and her home grown calla lilies make the perfect embellishment for the table's center arrangement. It's perfect.

When the doorbell rings she almost jumps out of her skin. *Why the nerves? These are my long-lost friends.* She peeks at the foyer mirror, moves a runaway hair back into place before opening the door.

From what she remembers of Marcie, Andrea instantly knows who the blond is smiling ear-to-ear on her porch. The whites of her eyes have a pink hue, as if she's been crying. Perhaps like Andrea, it's just shear exhaustion.

"Marcie? You haven't changed a bit!"

"Andrea! Well, I'd be lying if I said you hadn't changed!"

Andrea smiles. She knows exactly what she means. Converse sneakers, blue jeans and ponytail were her signature attire back in the day. These days her hair didn't make it past her earlobes and she didn't even own a pair of jeans.

As Marcie steps across the thresh-hold, Andrea jokes, "Did you expect me to be in a t-shirt and barefoot?"

"Or wearing boxing gloves!"

"Ah, you still have your sense of humor! Good. You made us laugh all of the time."

"Well, they say laughter is the best medicine for what ails us, right?"

"That's what they say."

In the dining room, Marcie asks, "How long have you been here?"

"Fifteen years. We just love it. I'll have to show you the back yard, but first, would you like a drink? I have Bellini mocktails."

"Mocktail? What's a mocktail? Sounds like a bird."

Marcie spreads out her arms and flaps them.

"Thanks for that visual," Andrea chuckles as the doorbell rings again. This time, with less apprehension, she heads toward it, yelling back to Marcie, "A mocktail is a cocktail without the alcohol! Isn't that a hoot?"

Charlie stands at the door with a flower bouquet. She holds it out.

"Andrea—I can't believe this day is finally here."

Although a little heavier, Charlie's as cute as Andrea remembers her. With a light embrace, she tries not to smash the flowers, and leads her into the house. In no time, they are so engaged in conversation it's is as if there had never been a thirty-five-year absence.

"So, Charlie, you're a social worker? How long have you been doing that?"

At this point, Andrea removes the covers from the trays of finger sandwiches, fruit salad, and her special homemade potato salad. With her hostess aura in full force, she scoops healthy portions on their plates. Charlie gives her a sheepish smile.

"What?" Andrea asks, "Too much?"

"I'm sorry, I'm trying to watch what I eat."

"I watch what I eat all the time," Marcie inserts. "From the time it leaves the plate to the moment I shove it in my mouth!"

They laugh. Andrea must admit, it feels good.

"Charlie, you didn't answer my question. How long have you been in that field?" she asks.

"Over twenty years."

"Twenty years? Holy cow. I don't think I've done anything for more than ten years," Marcie says and emphasizes ten with her hands. "And that kind of work I could never do."

"I love it. It's hard but it's worth it," Charlie responds.

Marcie shakes her head. "Don't you ever get tired of hearing people's problems all day? Or seeing the abuse and neglect? I think I'd rather be a trash collector."

Andrea almost chokes on a mouthful of potato.

"What? You'd rather collect people's material trash over their spiritual trash? Oh, and by the way you know they are called sanitation engineers? Can you believe that? Everyone must have a politically correct name. Don't want to offend anyone."

"Yeah, my favorite is *sandwich artist*. That was the person making my sub sandwich the other day!" Marcie mimes with her hands, becoming more animated as she stacks invisible layers of sandwich. Andrea thinks she sees her hands trembling, and asks, "Are you Italian, Marcie? You sure talk with your hands a lot!"

"Sometimes I feel like I'm an air traffic controller with my arms." Her arms shoot out as if to prove her point. That sets them all to laughing again.

After the meal, Andrea takes to cleaning up, refusing any help from Marcie or Charlie. Ever the hospitable hostess she says, "Please relax!" over and over, not taking her own advice.

The reunion is a success. Much better than she ever imagined. She wonders why they waited so long, but then remembers her own hesitation. But she has good reason. Maybe one day soon she'll tell them about it.

Wiping down the table, she looks out the French doors. It's time to show off her backyard haven.

"Ooh, I've got to show you outside. I know it's hot, but I've got to show you my pride and joy." They follow her like cattle while she tells of the various garden delights.

"I'm already envisioning my girls having their weddings here. We can either decorate the gazebo over there, and walk down the path here," she says, pointing to the locations in the yard. "They can say their vows under an arch by my magnolia tree or maybe by the fountain there! There are so many things we could do."

"Are any of your girls engaged?" Charlie asks.

"No, not yet. But time flies so fast. I expect that Reese will get married first. She's already twenty. I can't stand that boy she's dating, though. Oy! First of all, he's too old for her. And second, he's got this long hair and a ton of tattoos. She says she loves him. Right! I said that he's got to shave his hair and get rid of his tattoos before he can marry her. I don't think he'll do it. Who knows? So, we haven't even talked about your children. Do you have any?"

Both Marcie and Charlie shake their heads in unison as Charlie says, "I was diagnosed with endometriosis in my early twenties and then endometrial cancer in my early forties. I had a full hysterectomy after that."

Andrea says, "Oh, I'm sorry to hear that. How horrible. You cancer-free now?"

"I've been in remission for two years."

Charlie appears uncomfortable talking about it so Andrea addresses Marcie. "What about you? You don't have children either?"

Marcie gives what appears to be a look of regret and then says, "Seth and I wanted them for a while and tried to have children but I never got pregnant. And yada yada… after our tenth year trying, we finally gave up. We got more involved in his sister's children. We made a great auntie and uncle. And then a few years ago, we tried in vitro fertilization. I felt like a guinea pig and gave up on it after the first year.

"We thought maybe God had other plans for us so we researched fostering and we actually did that for about six months." Marcie stops suddenly as if in pain. She starts again.

"She was four years old and her name was Sophie. We fell in love with her and then her grandparents got custody of her. I don't think we anticipated how much pain it would cause us when she left. We decided then that fostering was out and maybe we should think about adoption. And then…" Marcie looks away.

Andrea must ask the question. "Are you going to adopt? You know there are all sorts of countries that have thousands of kids that need homes. China, Ethiopia, Liberia. The list goes on."

By now they are sitting on the bench underneath Andrea's favorite magnolia tree fanning themselves. Charlie gets up to inspect the garden pond and says, "You know, there are a lot of children that need to be adopted in the United States too. It's estimated that out of the almost half million children in the foster care system, there are about a quarter of a million of them waiting to be adopted. I don't know what ages you might consider but I could check some of my resources if you are seriously considering it."

As Marcie starts to answer, Andrea interrupts, "I wasn't saying that the U.S. doesn't have children that need adopting, I just meant that there are so many children around the world that will never have the opportunities that most children do here. I mean, we are the land of handouts, wouldn't you say? Do you see that a lot in your line of work? People on welfare? Food stamps? Well, they're not stamps now, are they? Anyway, we just seem to give out a lot to people that might not need it so much. I'm sure you see welfare fraud."

She has hit a nerve. Charlie's sweet face turns red and Andrea is positive it's not from the sun. As she watches her old friend sip her drink, she regrets her aggression.

Charlie says, "That's not the entire picture. Yes, I see a lot of people that need help. And most of the people I see do require some sort of assistance. And, yes, some of these parents make horrible choices in their lives, and perhaps out of those there are a few that we could perceive as playing the system. But I think that most people want to do the right thing and don't want to be on assistance. Or they don't know any other way."

There is an awkward silence until Marcie finally says, "We did talk about adoption before Seth and I separated a few months back. But I don't see where that's possible now. We're on the verge of divorcing."

This leaves room for another pause. Marcie finally smiles and says, "Well, I've made this a downer conversation. Who died here, huh? Let's talk about something else!" And with that they go back inside for dessert.

***

Cleaning up the rest of the dishes from the day's brunch, Andrea plays back the highlights of the reunion. But for the adoption faux pas, everything was a success. Her phone's vibration interrupts her elevation. It's Chris.

"How did it go?"

Still irritated by their last argument, she musters as much pleasantry as she can and says, "I think it went great." Suddenly Chris blurts out, "I want us to talk to someone. I can't keep going on like this pretending that everything is normal. We need to get counseling."

She sits, trying to think of something to say to meet him halfway without agreeing to counseling. She is just not willing to submit to being drilled on why she does the things she does. Her personal baggage is hers, and not some head doctor who probably is a deep seeded lunatic.

Aware Chris is waiting, she reaches for words that won't cause another fight. Negativity will only lead to more argument and she will never get him off her case. She finds herself looking in the corner of the room and spots a fresh spider web. On closer inspection, she can see that a spider has a tiny bug in its grasp. The bug is fighting for its life. How appropriate. She suddenly has empathy for the bug that she would normally stomp in a heartbeat. Like the bug, she feels as if she is suffocating, trapped and on the edge of ruin.

"Andrea? You there?"

Chris's voice snaps her to the issue at hand.

"I'm here. How about we talk when you get home?"

"Fine, but we are making a decision tonight."

Chris's resolve is something new.

"Okay, Chris. I will see you in a little bit. I love you."

"I love you too."

After she places her phone on the table, she grabs a paper towel and puts the bug out of its misery. Why delay the inevitable?

Chapter 13
~Marcie~

A light drizzle patters the sidewalk Sunday morning as Marcie stands
outside the hotel waiting for Charlie and Poppy. The week is over but
the dire events haunt her. Maybe extra prayers and kneeling at the
altar will produce a miracle. The shame is tying a knot in her
stomach. Something's going to give.

When Charlie and Poppy come out, Marcie waves.

"Hey, over here."

Charlie is attempting to cover Poppy's head with her hand. He
swats it away and softly hisses, "Will you knock it off? I'm not gonna
melt you know."

"I know, I know."

As Marcie grabs Poppy's hand, helping him into the front seat, she looks at Charlie, "How's everything?"

"Good," she sighs, "Pretty uneventful."

Marcie nods as if she understands her plight.

"I'm glad you decided to join me for church. I've been trying to go back regularly. It's usually hit or miss."

"The good Lord knows what's in your heart no matter where you're at," Poppy says.

This absolutely provides her no comfort since *the good Lord* is not happy with the state of her heart.

Poppy wheezes and Charlie talks about the hot weather as she takes a tissue and hands it to him. Watching the two interact, Marcie envies their relationship.

"But there's nothing like clouds in Florida," Poppy is saying, "It doesn't matter what kind either. Nimbus... cumulus... whatever type. God paints the most beautiful skies in Florida. No one can disagree with that."

Marcie smiles. "And don't forget cirrus. I used to call them *serious*! Until Charlie set me straight. Poppy, I've never been to Florida but I'm sure you're right. You used to live here in Virginia. Did you ever think Virginia's clouds were the best?"

"Nope. Never."

"So, I suppose that's why you left?" Marcie teases.

"I suppose that's as good a reason as any."

Charlie is quiet. Wanting to fill the empty air, Marcie offers up some information on Pastor Sinclair.

"I think you'll like Pastor Sinclair's sermons. He's been at Good Tidings Church for a few years now and everyone just loves him."

What would they would think if they knew Marcie was addicted to prescription drugs, obtained illegally, and that she spends so little time in church that Pastor Sinclair probably wouldn't even recognize her?

As soon as they arrive, Poppy says, "I've got to use the latrine. Where is it?"

Marcie shows them where the men's bathroom is and watches as Charlie walks Poppy to the door. Once Poppy has convinced Charlie that he can *take a leak* by himself, she returns.

"Marcie, it's been so great catching up with you and Andrea. I meant to ask you how your mother is doing. Gloria, right?"

"Mom's okay. We don't see each other a whole lot. She retired from the public school system a couple years ago and then dove into volunteering for every cause that comes her way. And yada yada…we never have been tight but we get along."

A look of surprise comes across Charlie's face. Marcie predicts her question.

"You're probably wondering why we aren't closer. It seems like we should be since we were the only ones each of us had after Daddy died."

"Yeah, I guess I was curious. I'm sorry to pry."

"I wasn't exactly the easiest teenager. I always struggled with school and those years were the worst. You remember how I almost drowned right before we met in first grade? I also had that head injury, which made it hard to concentrate on my schoolwork. The only thing that ever came natural to me was sports. Still does.

Anyway, I never became the kind of woman that my mom thought I should be. She was nurturing, a homemaker and wife, dainty, yada yada… and I was the opposite."

Charlie smiles politely and Marcie wonders if she can relate, but then remembers her mother wasn't in the picture when they met. She starts to ask about her when Poppy comes out of the bathroom looking somewhat relieved.

"I've got to sit down. My dogs are killing me," he mumbles as they move toward the sanctuary.

A few minutes after they are seated, the worship leader, who reminds Marcie of Liberace, stands up and leads an upbeat rendition of "How Great Thou Art" and she finds herself feeling a little optimistic as she sings. Minutes later they are listening to Pastor Sinclair begin the sermon.

"Join me this morning as we look at God's word from Psalm 27:1 through 6. You don't have to look far to see signs of trouble in the world today. Right? Every time we read the news, whether from a newspaper, radio, the internet, we see all sorts of stories of turmoil and problems people are facing."

She starts to zone out until the next words come out of his mouth.

"We will have anxieties in our lives, but what are we to do? 'Cast all of our anxieties on Him.' Sometimes we want quick solutions to the fear problem and answers to all of our anxieties, right? We're looking for a sense of security that will bring us peace in our hearts."

"Where do you look for that security? Do you look for it in your job? Some search for that reassurance in a relationship. Others place their trust in the government—well, maybe not so much today as years ago. What about drugs, alcohol, and so forth? Not one of these things I've mentioned is a real solution, is it? Because none of them offer total security or absolute reassurance. No amount of money, success, or any position in life can truly give you peace in every situation. So the question becomes, 'How can we have victory over fear?' The answer for us is given in Psalm 27, which says that we are to trust in God."

Marcie hangs on to every word, anticipating the next ones.

"As this psalm begins, David acknowledges his personal faith in God by using the pronoun 'my': He says 'My light, my salvation.' In times of darkness, do you look to God for light or are you content to be stuck in your uncertainty and stress?"

He pauses as he scans the congregation. His eyes land on her as he continues.

"One time or another you probably have walked into a room in total darkness. It's probably safe to say, everyone has felt caution, hesitation, and apprehension. Why is this? Because you are fearful about making a wrong turn or walking into something, right? But if the lights were on, this would not be the case, would it? Compare this to your life. When there are worrying times in which your fear is increased, you may not know which way to go or what to do. You are in the dark. David recognized that he had nothing to fear because the Lord was his light in dark and fearful times, right? And what's more, God was his salvation."

Marcie envisions David praying and entrusting his whole life to God. She's so wrapped up in her thoughts that she misses some of the sermon. When she breaks loose from the daydream, she concentrates on Pastor Sinclair again.

"David was able to ask the question: 'Whom shall I fear?' and he confessed God as the protection of his life. Which means He is a stronghold. A place of refuge. And David asks the question: 'Whom shall I dread?' But he has nothing to dread, does he? Nothing to dread about his enemies, or war. David's confidence was spoken from the experience of his life. Remember how he faced wild beasts? Remember how he faced the giant Goliath? What about the persecution from whole nations against him? He was always confident in God. This same confidence may be ours as well for David shows us how to obtain this for ourselves. Remember, forgetting what lies behind and reaching forward to what lies ahead, press on toward the goal for the prize of the upward."

She is so in tune with the sermon, that time races. And as the last "Amen" ends the morning service, a strange feeling strikes her. She can't quite put her finger on it, but the message somehow has made its way to her heart. She had heard many of Pastor Sinclair's sermons over the last couple of decades and many times walked out of the church not sure what his message meant. But this time was much different.

A hand touches her arm and she turns to see Mrs. Macklin squinting at her. She smiles wide, dentures glistening, as she points to Poppy.

"Missed you the other night, Marcie. Who are your friends?"

She's never seen Mrs. Macklin so excited. Giddy like an elementary school girl! She seems to be feeling a lot better than the last time they talked.

"Of course. Mrs. Macklin, this is a childhood friend of mine, Charlie. She's visiting with her grandfather, Moe Schramm."

And within minutes Poppy and Mrs. Macklin are talking as if they have known each other their whole lives. He invites Mrs. Macklin to join them for lunch at Millie's, a local dive, and she politely accepts with a silly grin on her face.

Millie's is a restaurant with a 1980's vintage décor, down home cooking, and karaoke starting at noon every Saturday and Sunday. It also happens to be the place that she met Seth. The memory sobers her.

After they eat plates of moist meatloaf, fluffy mashed potatoes and gravy, herbed green beans, and flaky rolls, Poppy and Mrs. Macklin join each other on stage for a seniors' rendition of a 1980s classic. Marcie feels like she's on a reality show that is a cross between a singing competition and matchmaking.

Mrs. Macklin and Poppy are singing "Islands in the Stream" and Marcie's mouth catches flies in disbelief. In the middle of her time warp, Charlie, who has also been moved by the turn of events, speaks first.

"Never in a million years would I have pictured my grandfather singing karaoke."

"And never in a million years would I have pictured not only Mrs. Macklin singing karaoke but her doing a duet with your grandfather!"

After they giggle at their synopsis of the cute new couple, Charlie asks, "How long have you been working at the gym?"

"About ten years. I was a teacher before that."

"Really?"

"Yeah. I guess it's hard to believe. I wasn't the sharpest tool in the shed."

Charlie looks embarrassed.

"No," she says, "I didn't mean anything like that. I guess I always pictured you doing something artistic. You loved to draw. Or something like what you're doing at the gym. Do you like what you do?"

Marcie hesitates. The morning has produced a throbbing headache that seems to be competing with her knee pain. She rubs her temples which doesn't go unnoticed by Charlie.

"You feeling okay?"

"I just have a lot on my mind."

"Do you want to talk about it?"

"You want to 'shrink' me?"

Charlie looks confused. She smiles sweetly.

"I'm a social worker, not a psychiatrist. I'm also a good listener."

"I'm sorry, Charlie. I haven't been feeling well."

And then Marcie does something unexpected. She isn't sure if it's due to the emotional reunion, Pastor Sinclair's sermon, or Charlie's calm nature, but she ends up telling her more than she imagined she would tell anyone. She tells her about the separation, Anthony's problems and the leave of absence from her job. She leaves out the prescription issue. After she unloads, she feels a weight has been lifted off her shoulders.

"What's going to happen with your friend Anthony?"

"I don't know. I haven't talked to him since his incarceration."

"If it's his first offense I would think that they would be lenient. Do you see you and Seth reconciling?"

It's a good question and Marcie takes a moment before she says, "If you had asked me that yesterday, I might have said no, but there was something about the message today that makes me think there may be some hope. Hopefully Seth hasn't changed his mind about it. He's been so patient with me."

Charlie nods and it seems like she wants to say something, but at that moment Mrs. Macklin and Poppy have come back to the table and their talk ends.

Chapter 14
~Charlie~

"I sure did like Mrs. Mackie." Marcie is pulling into Marvin's driveway when Poppy spills his heart. "I haven't felt this alive in a long time!" This time Charlie doesn't correct him by telling him that her name is Mrs. Macklin. It doesn't matter at this point.

Poppy has his duffle bag for his sleepover with Marvin. Charlie's looking forward to catch-up more with Marcie and Andrea.

"When can I see her again?"

Without hesitation she answers, "Why don't we all go out on Monday night? You, me, Marcie, Andrea, and Mrs. Macklin? Andrea's family could come too."

"That will be fine. I'd like that."

They do their usual routine with her grabbing his belt loop. As they stroll up the sidewalk to Marvin's house, the door opens. Marvin stands grinning like he's got miles of mischief planned out for the two of them. Standing behind him is a young woman named Margo, Marvin's housekeeper and cook.

After hugging Poppy and Marvin and a brief chat with Margo about some important medical matters, Charlie leaves Marvin's house feeling happy about her grandfather's adventure with his longtime friend.

Marcie is on her phone when Charlie reaches the car. She decides to check her own and sees a message from Mr. Jimenez. He asks to call him immediately and mentions that it is about the Taylor family. She dials his phone at once and he picks up on the first ring.

"Charlie."

"I just got your message. What's going on?"

"Hate to tell you this over the phone but it can't wait. Just received a call that Mr. Taylor shot his wife in their home this morning and she died a half-hour ago. The children weren't hurt. They were at a neighbor's house. They will stay there tonight. There are police detectives at the Taylor house now."

"Oh, my God. I can't believe it. That's awful. I thought they were making progress. He was going to counseling on a regular basis and getting his act together. What happened? Who are the detectives on the case?"

"Jesse Paterno and Lawrence Ramano."

Lawrence? Her heart aches. The huge burden she feels for the family overwhelms her, but the fact that Lawrence must investigate the tragedy, makes it worse. He can handle anything thrown his way, but in this case, he has gotten to know the Taylors through her. It's not his usual investigation of anonymity. He knows this family.

"I need you to pull their file and send me everything you've got. I know that you've been working on stuff there, so send me all of that as well. You'll be back Tuesday morning, right?"

"Yes, sir, I will."

"Charlie, I want you to prepare yourself for the questions that you will be asked. Read over all of the interviews, forms, visit notes—everything."

His persistence catches her by surprise. "Mr. Jimenez, are you concerned that I didn't follow up with something or didn't do my job properly?"

"Look, don't get all squirrelly on me. I know you're thorough. But the questions are going to be asked. I know you, Charlie. You are the best caseworker there is. Don't worry. And hang in there. I know that you cared for them."

"Yes, sir. Thank you."

When they hang up she notices the concerned look on Marcie's face. She can barely get the words out, "Mr. Taylor shot his wife," when she chokes on her tears. Marcie embraces her before pulling out of the driveway.

As they reach the end of the block she dials Lawrence.

"Hey, Charlie."

Hearing his voice, she lets out a long sigh.

"You okay?"

"Yes, I just wanted to hear your voice."

"I guess you heard about Mrs. Taylor. It's unbelievable. It must have shocked you. I know you had become close to her and the kids. The kids are fine. Are you going to be okay?"

"I'm still in shock, but I'll make it. I just can't believe it. This didn't have to happen. What's going to happen to Bella and Alicia? How about you? Are you still at the house?"

She pictures Lawrence walking through the house with his gloves and processing the scene methodically.

"I'm not gonna lie to you. It's been rough. Just grateful those girls weren't around. It could have been much worse. I can call you in a couple of hours. I'm glad you're there. I think it's best."

After they hang-up, Marcie agrees to take Charlie back to the hotel. Once inside her room, Charlie pulls out the Taylor paperwork and laptop. All the paperwork is in order. She notes the date she first met Mrs. Taylor, September 3, 2011. Mrs. Taylor had filed a restraining order against her husband. A couple of drunken binges had possessed him to rough her up and she finally decided to report him.

She remembers talking to him one night when he was sober and she was certain he was serious about seeking help.

"I'm gonna clean up my act," he said. "I need to be part of my girls' lives. Belly really needs me." He was referring to his four-year-old Down syndrome child.

And he did seek help for a while. He joined a church and went to self-help meetings and anger management classes. As far as she knew he only had one fallback. But that happened months ago.

Charlie gasps at the realization. Is it her fault? She was convinced there was hope for their reconciliation. Did she miss something? How did she get it all wrong after so many years of experience? Is she wrong to think she can help people with their problems?

A million thoughts race as she returns everything into organized piles and turns in for the night. Her very last thought as her head hits the pillow is of Lawrence.

Chapter 15
~Andrea~

Although, she's ready to have Marcie and Charlie over again, Andrea's nerves are frazzled. And because she refused to discuss their differences as promised, she and Chris haven't resolved anything. So she counts on her cleaning remedy to rid herself of the nervous energy.

While scrubbing the tile in the guest bathroom, it dawns on her she has yet to tell Chris of her latest conversation with Maggie Ryan and *All Fed Up*. And he never asked. Another reason to scrub.

Forge ahead. Chin up. Put the past behind her. Suck it up. On to bigger and better. It's meant to be. All of the other quotes she used since childhood to cope. She's good at it most times. Besides, a better job will open up and *All Fed Up* will be sorry they didn't snatch her up when they had the chance.

After a few more meaningful scrubs at the grout, she gathers the cleaning supplies and puts them away. In the hallway, the anxiety returns at the sight of the closed door to the spare bedroom. They haven't had guests in a long time, and ever since she placed her mother's belongings in there, it didn't seem like the room would ever be used again. The room became a shrine to her mother.

As much as her thoughts tell her to stay put, her body seems to have a mind of its own and soon the door is open. The hundreds of items salvaged from the estate are stored neatly in stacked boxes and placed systematically around the room, just as she left them. Andrea didn't know what she was going to do with all of it, she just didn't want to get rid of it. The guest bed is full of more treasures—folded antique quilts, dusty framed pictures. And worn picture albums.

Cautiously walking through the room, she touches the boxes as if the action will resurrect her mother. Funny how a whole lifetime can be condensed into a few boxes. She moves the pictures and sits down. Her bottom barely hits the bed when she hears, "What are you doing?" Startled, she looks up to see Reese at the doorway.

"You scared the heart out of me! What are you doing here? I thought you and Adrian were going off together."

"We got in an argument and I told him to take me home."

"Well, that figures. Are you starting to see that maybe he's just not right for you?"

"Mom, it wasn't anything bad. We just didn't agree on something. No big deal. We were discussing you and how hard you are on me. And how you don't see us as a real couple."

Reese looks exasperated and sits next to Andrea on the bed.

Andrea smirks. "I'm sure he agreed with every awful word you said about me."

"Actually, Mom, you'll be glad to know that he agrees with you. He thinks I shouldn't disrespect you. And he thinks that we're too young to get too serious. He actually thinks that we should take our relationship slower. So what do you think of that?"

She didn't see that one coming. It must be bogus. Like an Eddie Haskell moment. He probably always says the right things for the parents' benefit but inside he's a juvenile delinquent.

"I think that he's trying to win me over."

"Of course you think that. I obviously can't have a healthy relationship with anyone. Is that what you think Mom? Just because you've got issues I can't possibly have anything normal?"

Reese's words aren't sarcastic. They're sad. And then apologetically she says, "I'm sorry, Mom. I just wish you would get help."

"I'm fine. You know that's not good for a relationship."

Reese looks at her quizzically. "What?"

"Not talking things out."

"Uh huh." Reese says.

"What's that supposed to mean?"

Reese mumbles and walks away. Her loose curls bob slightly and for a moment it reminds Andrea of when she was a toddler. She decides to let her go, but is left wondering what she meant. After one more scan of the room, she closes the door and remembers Marcie's invitation to church on Sunday. While Andrea had politely declined, she still was interested in learning about it. She runs upstairs to find out more about Good Tidings on the internet.

Chapter 16
~Marcie~

"**I** really wish I could have attended yesterday. Maybe another time? I'm thrilled both of you could be here today though. Oh, I've got to show you something," Andrea says excitedly as she pours tea into their glasses.

She has once again provided awesome food, and Marcie starts to thank her, when Andrea blurts, "Remember the picture I posted of us? Well, I found it when I was going through my mothers' things last year. There were other pictures too. Hold on a sec."

She dashes off leaving Marcie and Charlie wide-eyed. Within a minute or so she's back with a worn picture album.

"I tell you…when I went through my mother's things, I had to put on gloves, some of the items were so…" her words trail off.

Marcie leans in as Andrea sets the book on the marble table.

"Most of these pictures I hadn't seen since graduation. I think she must have forgotten she had them."

As soon she sees the first picture she catches Andrea's excitement. Andrea is holding a plaid blanket pretending to be a matador while Charlie is running at her with fingers to her head like bulls' horns. Marcie is the rodeo clown.

They laugh and carry on like old times as they work through all of the silly moments setting up scenes and taking pictures with Andrea's mom's Polaroid and reminisce over each pose and scene. Almost an hour later they are at the end with only a couple of pages left. Andrea suddenly jumps up.

"Hold on a minute. I remember that there was another book," and off she goes upstairs again.

In between chuckles, Marcie says, "It must be really good!"

They flip the last page and a piece of paper falls to the ground. It's an old news article folded in half. Marcie cranes her neck as Charlie unfolds it and places the musty paper on the table between them. The article, "MAN KILLED BY AUTOMOBILE WHILE JOGGING," is dated August 27, 1972.

In a matter of seconds the happiness switches to somberness. Charlie gasps and covers her mouth. Neither says a word as they study the grainy black and white picture of the car that hit the jogger.

Oblivious to what just transpired, Andrea comes charging in with another book to show. "I found it," she says triumphantly. Marcie and Charlie just stare.

Andrea sets the second album on the table and says, "What's going on? You both look like you've seen a ghost."

Charlie finally says, "We found a story," and points to the article on the table. Marcie remains frozen as if the words on the page have time-warped her to that decade.

> A high school teacher has died from
> injuries he suffered after a reckless car
> hit the man while he was jogging. Gary
> Stokes was jogging early Sunday morning
> when a drunk driver in a forest green 1970
> Ford Maverick driving erratically down
> Collins Avenue struck Mr. Stokes from the
> side. The driver was driving on a suspended
> license.
> Mr. Stokes leaves behind one daughter
> and his wife of ten years and many students
> that he called his kids at Granby High
> School.

A woman's name is handwritten in the right margin with an arrow pointing to the photo of the green 1970 Ford maverick.

The awful sensations haunting Marcie for the last few months are now in full force. She feels like she will pass out, but finds the nerve to ask, "Who's Linda Schramm?"

"I have no idea. I don't remember that name," Andrea says. "Charlie, do you remember?"

Charlie whispers, "That was my mother."

"Your mother?" Andrea asks with the same shock that Marcie feels. She mumbles, "I thought your mother's last name was Baldwin."

"From what I understand, after my mother divorced my father, she went back to her maiden name."

At this point Marcie isn't even sure why she asked. She doesn't even care. She wants to scream, *What does it matter? Your mother killed my dad!*

While Charlie is explaining to Andrea about her childhood,

Marcie feels the blood drain from her face.

"Marcie, are you going to be okay?"

She starts to sit to shake the dizziness. Beads of sweat trickle across her forehead. The floor seems to be collapsing from under her as she falls to the ground.

Everything is spinning and turning dark and she feels like she is a little girl again. She's six years old playing in the beach sand with her father. They are laughing, but something is wrong. She's not in the sand; it's water and its tossing her back and forth. She's going to be sick.

"Something's really wrong, Andrea. Call 911 now!" someone yells. Marcie throws up violently on the floor and then tries to get up but is too weak.

"No, Marcie." She thinks it's Charlie. "Stay down, okay?"

"Okay," she mumbles, but she's so confused. *Where am I?*

She's six again and this time on the third floor apartment on Collins Avenue, looking down at the street. She's sad as she looks for her father.

It's still dark but she finally sees him under the lamppost. He's running on the sidewalk. He waves and smiles as he sees her. He's coming home! But another object comes into view. It's a car heading straight for him. *No! No! Daddy, move!*

Marcie opens her eyes and Charlie is kneeling next to her and places a wet washcloth on her forehead as she says, "Just try to relax. The ambulance is on the way. I want to prop this pillow behind you so you can lie on your side. Can you talk to me? I need you to say something."

It's at this point that Marcie realizes she is struggling to catch her breath. She then panics more as she realizes what comes out of her mouth doesn't match what's in her thoughts.

Charlie whispers, "It's okay. You're going to be okay."

Chapter 17
~Charlie~

*T*he ambulance speeds off leaving Andrea and Charlie standing by the front door overwhelmed and frightened by the events of the afternoon. Charlie slides her arm around Andrea's waist, hugging her lightly. "She'll be okay."

Andrea nods and mumbles, "She will," and walks toward the kitchen.

Confused by Andrea's reaction, Charlie grabs her keys and purse from the table and says, "Come on. Let's go. I'll drive."

"I can't go. I need to clean up."

Did she hear her right? Suddenly, Andrea looks very fragile.

"What do you mean?"

"I just can't go right now. I need to be here when Rochelle gets home. I've got to get dinner ready."

She still can't believe her ears. Andrea's reaction seems so…blasé. Surely Reese can pick Rochelle up or she can make some other arrangements. Andrea's response disappoints her.

"Can't Reese pick her up?"

"No. Look, I really can't go. I'm sure you can explain it to her. And tell her I may come by later with Chris."

Charlie feels her face burning, certain it's beet red. *How can Andrea call herself a friend and be so uncaring?* She walks toward the front door saying with frustration, "She may have had a heart attack or something. I would think that your family would be understanding and help out."

As she opens the door to leave, Andrea comes up behind her and shuts it. Startled, Charlie waits.

Gradually, Andrea says, "I can't because I can't leave the house."

"Andrea, you can ride with me. Your family can help you out with Rochelle."

"No, you don't understand. If I could, I would."

"You're speaking in riddles. What don't I understand?"

Andrea looks away. "I haven't left the house in a year."

As she processes the admission, Charlie can't believe it. Thoughts ping-pong their way around her head. *Was she ill? Was she held against her will? Surely she's not afraid. How did this happen? How did she not pick up on this? Is she slipping…again?*

"What happened? Can you tell me?"

"I don't want to talk about it now. You need to go. I'll call you later," Andrea answers abruptly.

Charlie begins to insist, but thinks better of it and decides to abide by her wishes. After all, it must have taken a lot of courage for Andrea to tell her. She hugs her and leaves with a promise, "I'll call you when I find out something about Marcie."

As she walks dismally to her car, she digests Andrea's candid exposure. She never had anyone close to her with agoraphobia. There was a man she met who was in a custody battle with his wife, and he hadn't left the house in five years. The man always reminded her of a younger version of Poppy.

When she reaches the corner stop sign, she thinks fondly about the man. His name was Cal and although he seemed to have a rough exterior he treated his children with immense love and support. Unfortunately that wasn't enough and the court ruled that he wasn't fit to have custody of his children. Charlie later learned his agoraphobia was only a small portion of his mental instability and that he eventually committed suicide.

At the thought of his demise, she grips the steering wheel with uncertainty. Every ounce of her wants to drag Andrea out of there and rush to see Marcie. But would that make Andrea frantic? What if she despises her and ends their friendship?

What about me? With this fresh exposure of their past, this surely will put her in a different light in Marcie's eyes. That could be another friendship ending.

Suddenly a horn blares, snapping her back, and she immediately knows what she needs to do. Her heart blinds the logical part of her brain and she makes an illegal U-turn at the stop sign and heads back to Andrea's house.

She pulls into the driveway and shuts off her car. Closing her eyes, she prays for the right words to say. With wavering confidence she opens them, marches to the front door with conviction, and presses the doorbell. When Andrea doesn't answer she grows more concerned. She rings again. Still no answer. After a third time, she remembers Andrea's favorite spot underneath the magnolia tree.

Walking to the back of the house she pieces together what she wants to say. As she thought, Andrea is sitting on the garden bench under the tree, as if in a trance.

"Andrea?"

She looks up, frightened. "I thought you left."

"I changed my mind. You're coming with me. You can do this, Andrea, and I'm going to help you."

Andrea shakes her head with the same conviction minutes earlier.

"Charlie, you are wasting your time. I told you that I can't go. This isn't easy for me. Now you know what a phony I am, huh? Tough as nails but can't even go to the store to buy them."

"I have no idea what you are going through, but I know that it's not easy. And I want to help you through it. I know that you can get into that car and go to the hospital to see our friend."

"It's not going to work. Chris and my girls have tried many times. I am not ready."

Charlie sits next to her dear friend. *God, please give me the strength and courage to know what to say to Andrea.*

A few more seconds pass and then she remembers the Bible verse that Marcie's pastor preached days earlier. *The Lord is my light and my salvation; Whom shall I fear? The Lord is the strength of my life; Of whom shall I be afraid?*

She knows exactly what she needs to say.

"Andrea, you know I'm frightened too."

"What do you mean?"

"I mean, about going to the hospital and what Marcie is going to think. This was all a shock to me too. I never realized that my mother was the drunk driver who killed her father."

Andrea ponders this for a moment before she says, "You've got to know that wasn't your fault and you had nothing to do with it."

"But I don't know she's convinced of that. It makes me scared, but I know that God can lead me into the right path, into light, not darkness. Remember the verse Marcie shared with us the other night?"

Charlie senses Andrea's uneasiness stirring and for a second thinks she's going back to the house. But she doesn't.

"I don't know if I believe that. It's been so long since I actually had faith. Even when I was attending church last year, I can't say that I really bought all of the stuff that the church was peddling. I really went because I wanted something positive in the girls' lives to help in raising them and keep them out of trouble."

"That's a start."

"I think it was when my mother died a couple of years ago that I lost what faith I had."

Charlie smiles. "I'm not super spiritual but the Bible says that you only need a little bit of faith... the faith of a mustard seed."

"What if I have a panic attack?"

"Well, at least you'll be in a good place. And I'm here for you too."

Still not sure Andrea is convinced, Charlie holds out her hand and says, "I'll be right by your side. I promise you."

Chapter 17
~Andrea~

Sitting in the hospital waiting room, Andrea's convinced her heart will explode. Her trembling hands tell on her until Charlie gently puts hers on top, stifling them.

"You're going to be okay. We're halfway through. Look how far you've made it."

Andrea nods and looks at the ground, hoping a magic trap door will transport her safely to her kitchen. After a few more minutes of apprehension, she raises her head.

"Do you remember my mom, Tina?"

"Of course. I loved her. She was awesome. I couldn't wait to go over to your house and play. Your mom always let us do anything…or eat anything! And I remember that chocolate mayonnaise cake she made all the time. Why?"

She sips the water on the end table next to her before she says, "Did you ever notice anything strange about our house or my mom?"

"Well, you did have a lot of stuff. I remember that for sure. I remember she collected stuff like those big buttons, and music albums, and tree ornaments! Which I always thought was strange since you were Jewish, weren't you?"

"My father was Jewish, my mother was Protestant. It seems we settled to the *goy* side. And boy did she like to collect everything."

She sucks in deeply before letting out a sigh. It relaxes her a bit.

"She had a big problem with collecting. It got worse as we grew older. It drove my dad crazy. Don't you remember having to step over stuff? Well, it got to the point that I had to move into my brothers' room until they moved out. Talk about awkward…" She wipes the sweat on her neck. She must look a mess.

Charlie digs in her purse and finds a pack of tissues and hands it to her. As Andrea blots her brow and neck she says, "I was sixteen when my dad died. Mom totally went off the deep end and it was awful. I think that he had helped her keep it together for us, but once he was gone there was really no one who could do that for her."

Charlie's eyes are helplessly looking at her. There's something calming in them. She's seen a lot too.

"She put all of her time and energy in making everyone happy except herself. What everyone didn't know was that she had mental problems she hid. Bi-polar and OCD weren't household topics back then. So she let people think that she was just a messy housekeeper, but it was far worse than that."

She takes another sip to relieve her dry mouth.

"When I first noticed something was wrong, I think I was thirteen. She'd be up all night arranging her collections, talking to herself, working herself to death. The next morning she'd act as if nothing was wrong. Then a couple of days later she'd stay in her room all day by herself—not talk to anyone. As great as my mom was, she was that crazy. I was afraid that I was going to be just like her. I think that she kept most of it hidden from the outside world pretty well. But when Dad died, I don't think that she could handle it anymore. She gave up on life, including the dance studio. I know it absolutely killed her. And things spiraled from there."

The shaking starts again and her stomach aches, but she's determined to get everything out of her system.

"As much as I loved her, I swore to myself that I was not going to be like her and I made it my life's mission to be the total opposite. But God had different plans for me and the little red apple didn't fall far from the tree. As much as I've tried to be 'normal,' normal was not in the cards for me. I thought if I kept my house the cleanest, my family the smartest and most organized and my girls the prettiest that it would make all of the other thoughts in my head go away. And I kept things hidden from the world for a long time… except for Chris. He knew I was messed up all along. And he still stayed with me. Go figure!"

She glances around the empty waiting room as Charlie pats her hand again before grabbing her empty cup. "Let me get you some more water."

She walks to the water cooler and Andrea wonders what she could possibly be thinking. This is more than she ever imagined that she would reveal to anyone. As she returns, tears are flowing down Andrea's face.

"Andrea, are you all right? You don't have to say any more. Do you want me to call Chris now?"

"I'll be okay." She takes another tissue, determined to get the whole story out. "I've made it this far and I want to see Marcie."

"I'm so proud of you. I know how incredibly difficult this has been."

"Well, I wouldn't have done this if it weren't for you. Thank you," she whispers.

A couple of minutes pass before the courage strikes her again.

"It was a few years ago when I knew things were unraveling. I was forty-two and having some midlife crisis. The first moment I knew something was wrong was when I had an anxiety attack while I was grocery shopping. I was at the register paying for my things when it struck. Thankfully I was able to make it to my car and get home. The second time I wasn't so lucky. I was at work and had a terrible attack again. My boss thought I was having a stroke—which I wasn't—and he called an ambulance. I remember going home from the ER feeling so embarrassed."

"How horrible for you," Charlie interjects.

"It was. The third time happened shortly after my mom died a little over a year ago. I was at a store again. This time it was a department store. By that time I had already started to limit how much I was going out. I stopped going out with friends and family, and eventually stopped going to church. It's amazing how easy it was for me to get used to staying home in my safe haven."

Charlie nods again sympathetically but Andrea's sure she can't believe how she got to such a low point in her life. Between the three of them, Andrea was always the bravest.

"And then it got to the point that I wasn't leaving the house at all. Just like that. I had no desire to see anyone or do anything outside the fortress that I built. I stopped working for the company that I had been with for ten years. And then I didn't work at anything for about six weeks. But I went stir-crazy. I've always found great pleasure in working. So I started my own graphic arts design business from home and that was doing pretty well at first but has fizzled.

"It's been a tough road for me but I can't make up for what it has done to my family. They don't say much about it anymore, because they never know how I'll respond. When Chris has tried, I bite his head off. It's like they don't know who this crazy woman is in their house and sometimes I don't know either. And I don't know how to fix this. I swear I don't want things to be this way." She pauses to catch her breath, but starts to hyperventilate.

Charlie notices her plight immediately. "You're doing great. Take a couple of slow deep breaths. You're going to be fine."

Andrea takes her advice and within a couple of minutes the wave of anxiety subsides.

"Do you want me to call Chris?" Charlie asks.

"No, I'll do it. Thanks though."

She reaches for her phone and quickly texts Chris. Charlie stares at her. Andrea smiles weakly.

"I'm okay."

"I know. Andrea, do you remember how we met?"

"Of course. It was at my mother's studio. You were just starting dance lessons and I met you one afternoon after school. You were so quiet."

Charlie nods. "I was meek as a mouse. I remember Poppy had taken me and I was scared to death. I begged him to stay with me but he wouldn't. My mother had abandoned me and he had just started to take care of me. To say I was insecure would be an understatement. But I remember meeting you like it was yesterday. You were so confident and sure of yourself. I thought you were much older. You always acted older than everyone."

They sit reminiscing until Andrea looks at her watch. It's been almost two hours since they arrived. She starts to ask Charlie if they should talk to a nurse again but stops when she sees a short, balding man with a goatee smiling at her. He walks toward them and in an instant she realizes it's Seth.

"Andrea?" He holds out his hand. Andrea shakes it and says, "Seth?"

"Yes. Good to meet you." He turns to Charlie. "And you must be Charlie?"

Charlie nods. "Hi. It's very nice to meet you. How's Marcie?"

"She's going to be okay. She had a mild heart attack but with some rest and medicine she won't need any surgery. I hate to think if you both weren't with her. I haven't even been able to talk with her yet—she's sleeping."

Andrea's speechless, which seems to be happening a lot lately. Charlie manages to say, "I can't believe it. She seems so healthy. Is there anything that we can do?"

"Pray for her recovery. Pray for us. She must have told you we're separated?"

Andrea thinks of her own marriage. "She did. We're sorry for what you both are going through."

A cell phone buzzes and by the time Charlie realizes it's hers, she can't reach it quick enough to answer. Within seconds of retrieving it, a concerned look comes over her face.

"What could Marvin be calling me for? Let me give him a call real quick."

She taps the buttons on her phone and waits for a response.

"Marvin, this is Charlie. Is something wrong with Poppy?"

Her face contorts into concern .

"Well, I'm actually at the hospital right now," she finally says. She nods and then adds, "I'll be right there."

Andrea aches for her friend. If something happens to Poppy, Charlie will be devastated.

After she hangs up, she blurts, "I'm so sorry. I need to go to the Emergency Room. Poppy may have broken his leg. Marvin brought him in." She addresses Andrea. "Are you going to be okay?"

Andrea's not sure if she can handle being by herself, but she certainly doesn't want to burden Charlie any further. Thankfully, Seth pipes in. "You know Marcie will probably be sleeping for a little bit. I can tell her you both were out here and that you'll be back later."

They hug Seth and Andrea says, "I will be praying for you and Marcie." And this time she means it.

After they say their goodbyes, they race down the corridors of the hospital to find Poppy.

Chapter 18
~Marcie~

*T*he pills tease her. She wants to grab them but her conscience is telling her it isn't the right time. There are so many bottles. She didn't realize it was this bad. Charlie is in a chair by the window looking the other way. So easy to sneak just one but she's scared.

Seth reads the newspaper. He speaks softly to Charlie but Marcie can't make out what he's saying. They look over at her and then whisper again. Certainly they're talking about her. *What are they saying? What are they doing here?* She's having problems with her words again. Charlie gets up and looks at her with disgust and walks away. Seth doesn't even bother looking up. *What is happening?*

Marcie awakens.

The room is dark except for light underneath the door and the hospital monitor by the bed. A slight hum and steady beeping comes from the machine. After her eyes adjust, she sees a sleeping figure slumped in a chair. Seth.

She tries clearing the cobwebs out of her head to figure out what she is doing in the hospital bed. It comes back to her and she remembers fainting at Andrea's house. Seth moves in the chair.

"Marcie?"

"Hey."

"How you feeling?"

"Okay. My head and chest are killing me. What happened?"

"You had a heart attack."

As the shock of his words settles in her mind, he gets up and sits on the bed.

"Charlie and Andreas' quick actions really saved you."

"Where are they?"

"Charlie's grandfather is in the ER so they went to make sure he's okay. They seem really nice. They were very concerned about you."

She thinks about Charlie and Andrea and what brought on the episode and starts to cry.

"Honey, it's okay. You're going to be fine. You don't need any surgery. The doctor said it was a mild heart attack. Medicine and taking better care of you is what he was saying…"

"That's not why I'm crying. Although I can't believe it. I'm only forty-five. I'm too young for a heart attack."

"You think this is a wake-up call?" he asks.

"Maybe. Look, Seth… about us… I think that—"

"We don't need to talk right now about it," Seth interrupts. "You need your rest. Try to go back to sleep."

But she can't let it go and shakes her head. "No, I need to tell you this. I've really messed up lately. I need to get my life straight. I've been so out of control. I need to stop the pills I was taking. I need you back."

"I need you too, Marcie. I've always needed you." He kisses her hand and says, "We don't have to have children if you don't want them. I just want us to be together. My life isn't the same without you."

While she never thought she would say the next sentence, she knows she means it with every fiber of her being.

"I do want children. I just get scared when I think of being responsible for another life. I mean, look what I've done to my life. That's why I needed to get away. I wasn't running away from you. I was trying to run away from me—which I know sounds ridiculous— because I knew if I stayed with you I would hurt you even more. My biggest fear is that I will be an awful mother. And worse yet, what if something happens to me? Or you? And then this child has the rest of his or her life thinking about not having us around."

"You're getting way ahead of us. You're killing us off without us even having a chance at parenthood. Life is so much bigger than us. God is much bigger than us. Remember that."

She breathes deeply and is shocked again by the soreness in her chest. She tries to relax but her breathing feels labored. Ignoring the discomfort, she says, "And I want to adopt like you talked about."

Seth's face lights up. "I want you to get better and not think about anything else right now but resting, okay? Will you promise me that? We have plenty of time to talk later."

Marcie nods. "But we need to talk about this soon. Life is too short. We need to find out what we need to do to adopt. And I need to tell you something else. Remember Anthony from the gym?"

"Yeah."

"I was getting painkillers from him. And now he's in big trouble. He was in jail but Kesha helped him get out. I don't know where he's at now. That's just like Kesha to help. She's wanted to help me for a while but I've been refusing her every time."

It's amazing the relief that is felt by an honest confession. Seth doesn't even seem a bit surprised. It's as if he was waiting for a long time for her to tell him this.

"Let's take this one step at a time," She hears him say just as she drifts to sleep.

Chapter 19
~Charlie~

𝓗alfway to finding Poppy, Chris catches up to them down one of the corridors and takes Andrea home. By the time Charlie makes it to the ER, she is told Poppy has already been taken to one of the exam rooms.

She feels frantic, something she's not accustomed to feeling. As she rounds the bend toward his room, she hears his voice.

"Charlie," he yells playfully as she enters. This is a good sign.

A nurse is taking a blood sample. She smiles and whispers, "Shh… Mr. Schramm…" and gives Charlie a wink. She's probably fallen for his antics and Charlie can't imagine what he's already said or done.

"Oh, Charlie, you aren't going to believe what happened. I was at Marvin's…" His arm stretches out as he points to Marvin standing in the corner. Marvin gives a sheepish grin.

"Hi, Marvin. Hi, Poppy." She gives each of the men a kiss. "So what happened?"

"Marvin and I went for a walk around his neighborhood."

"Poppy, do you think that you should have done that with your back?"

"Well, I did fine on the walk. I fell when we came back from the walk! We went to Marvin's deck and I fell right down the steps!"

Regret seeps in Marvin's face. "I'm sorry, Charlie. I tried to catch him."

Poppy responds, "What are you apologizing to Charlie for? I'm the one that fell!"

"I know that, you old goat!"

They seem to enjoy their banter back and forth. Charlie can clearly see they have missed one another and Poppy is more lucid than he's been in weeks.

After a few more jabs at each other, Marvin leaves once Charlie promises to keep him informed of Poppy's progress. Once the door shuts, Poppy lets his guard down and she sees he is in more pain than he let on as he winces moving his leg. "Marvin said you were already at the hospital? For what?"

"Marcie had a heart attack. The doctor told her husband that she will be fine though. Thank goodness."

"A heart attack? She's too young for that! Well, that's good she's going to be fine."

Poppy seems to have more on his mind.

"Did you talk about anything interesting? Did you talk about your childhood?"

He knows that she knows.

"We talked a little. Andrea showed us an old photo album that was her mother's. Her mother died last year and she had just recently started going through some of her stuff. As we were going through the album, it started out fun as we talked about all of the stuff we used to do. Then we saw the article. Poppy, I know that my mother killed Marcie's father in the car accident."

He closes his eyes. "I always meant to say something to you but I never knew what would be the best thing to say. I didn't want to upset you." One lone tear rolls down his cheek.

"Poppy, don't. It's okay. We'll talk about it later."

"You don't understand. There is more that you don't know. I want to tell you about your mother."

This is a first. Poppy never opens up about her mother. It's always a subject that they manage to bypass. Charlie squirms nervously in her seat unprepared for this long awaited day.

Poppy seems to have changed his mind as he remains still, but Charlie realizes he is trying to put his thoughts together.

"My Dear and I gave your mother a good life. She was happy at one time. And smart. And, boy, could she dance. She was a little ballerina! She could have gone to… what was the name of that school… uh… Juilliard! Yes, she could have gone there if she wanted. But one day that all changed. Your mother was… I think… seventeen years old and had gone to a friend's house one night. Patty. Yes, I'm certain Patty was her name."

He pauses as if the memory is too much to bear.

"She was supposed to spend the night but she never was one to do well on sleepovers and she decided to come back home. It was one o'clock in the morning. I was overseas back then and she didn't want to make My Dear come get her so she decided to walk home. It was only a few blocks away from our home. From what I understand she didn't even see the two monsters coming." Poppy chokes up.

"Poppy, you don't need to talk about this now. When you're feeling better you can tell me."

He shakes his head and after several more seconds is able to say, "You need to know why she did what she did."

At this point, she is conflicted, not sure if she is ready for it. Luckily, the nurse returns, giving Charlie time to digest Poppy's words. The nurse checks his monitor and vitals and exits with, "The doctor will be in soon, Mr. Schramm."

Poppy doesn't miss a beat. "So these two horrible animals... two punks wandering through the neighborhood... came up behind her and attacked her viciously. They dragged her to a wooded area between Patty's home and ours. They treated her like she was lower than dirt. They beat her... and raped her... and left her for dead. Your mother almost died that night."

Charlie wants him to stop.

"I don't understand why you're telling me."

"I'm getting to it. Once your mother recovered we could see that she became this different person. She never got over what happened to her. She didn't care about anything anymore... not her dance... not My Dear... not me. And she started to drink with that Patty girl. She became a wild child. Then she left our home. I think she was eighteen."

For a few seconds, Poppy loses his train of thought, and Charlie is ready to bolt from the room. But then he starts up again.

"We didn't hear from her again until she was pregnant with you. She came home and asked for our help. My Dear convinced me to take her back. I did and for a while there was hope. She actually stayed clean through the pregnancy. We thought that she was moving on with her life. Even after you were born, she stayed sober for two years. That's when she eloped with your father but it didn't last. Then those boys finally went to trial. And it must have brought back all of the hell she had gone through. She went downhill again."

At this point she realizes she's crying too. All her life she thought of her mother as a character in someone else's story; a person without feelings and heart. As Poppy talks about her, she puts together the pieces of puzzle that make up her mother. In the inner part, is a teenager full of hope and a lover of life. She pictures her mother kissing her parents goodnight and laughing with her friends. Then, her mother is dancing with joy. It suddenly dawns on Charlie the reason her mother wanted her to take dance lessons.

The frame of the puzzle is her mother's pain. The pain of losing her innocence, security and trust in mankind. The frame molds the rest of her life.

Poppy interrupts her train of thought, "She avoided us like the plague. Her drinking took a front seat. We would try to keep track of where she was living, but she moved so often it was impossible to know where she was. Finally she seemed to settle in an apartment where she knew the landlord. By then My Dear was sick with the cancer that took her to be with the Lord. Your mother never got to see her before she died. I was so angry with your mother and I've held on to that anger for a long time. I don't want to go to my grave being angry at her anymore."

Poppy sobs. Charlie holds him, attempting to comfort the years of built up regret and sadness, and she realizes she needs comforting herself.

"It wasn't long after My Dear died that I knew I had to save you from that life. There was no one else that could do that but me. No one. I planned to talk to your mother first but when I called the apartment there was no answer. It was getting late and I just had a suspicion something was wrong. I went over to the apartment and found you there by yourself. You were hungry and scared and needing a bath. I swore you would never go back there again."

He sighs and rubs his injured leg. In a couple of minutes, he answers the question that has built up in her mind.

"I was going to confront her the next morning. I woke up early like usual. You were sleeping in my bedroom with your cat, Moses. I remember making coffee and getting the newspaper off the porch. I was thinking about what I was going to say to her when I unrolled the newspaper and got the shock of my life. There on the bottom of the front page was the car I gave your mother. She was driving it when she hit Mr. Stokes."

She pictures Poppy's grief as he opened the newspaper that morning expecting to read the news like normal, only to find out that his one and only daughter made the news.

"I was beside myself, Charlie. I didn't know what to do. When you finally woke up, I took you to Mrs. Fishkin's dance studio. I asked her to watch you for me. I needed some time to find your mother. After I dropped you off, I went to your mother's apartment first. She wasn't there. Then I checked at a local bar she hung out at. I looked all day. No one had seen her. At the end of the day, I went back to her apartment—I was going to wait for her to return. The door was unlocked this time."

Charlie remembers the very moment he is talking about when he took her to the dance studio. She had no idea at the time everything that had transpired. Before she has a chance to respond, a young doctor comes in with an x-ray.

"Well, Mr. Schramm, you broke your leg in two areas." As the doctor proceeds to give the details of Poppy's diagnosis and recovery time, Charlie drifts to that day.

***

1972

The girls in the mirrored room danced in unison to a song that reminded her of music Poppy played on his record player. She wanted to dance too, but it felt like her feet were stuck in mud.

Besides, she really had to go to the bathroom.

Poppy was talking to Mrs. Fishkin about something important. She could tell it was adult talk by the serious look on his face and knew not to disturb him. He looked upset too. But she couldn't wait long. She crossed one leg in front of the other as she hoped he would see her. As she stood at the door in awe of the dancing girls in their colorful costumes, she sensed someone behind her and turned around to see two girls staring.

The blond girl smiled while the taller girl asked, "Who are you?"

She glanced back to make sure the tall girl was talking to her. When she saw no one else she said, "Charlie."

"Charlie? That's a boy's name. Your name can't be Charlie."

Charlie blushed.

The smaller girl then spoke up, "I like your name. It's kind of close to mine. My name's Marcie. She's Andrea."

"Hi," Charlie whispered.

"Do you have to tinkle?" Marcie asked. Charlie blushed again, straightened her legs and managed to utter, "Yes."

Marcie grabbed her hand and led her past Poppy, who looked down suspiciously at them. He stopped talking to Mrs. Fishkin and asked, "Charlie, who are your friends?"

She was about to answer when Andrea piped in, "I'm Andrea and this is Marcie," and then she pointed to Mrs. Fishkin and said, "She's my mom. Charlie said she has to go to the bathroom." And with that the three of them walked toward the back of the studio leaving the two adults to their discussion.

After she finished in the bathroom, she found Marcie and

Andrea playing "Miss Mary Mack" outside the bathroom door. In the short time that she had been in there, they had managed to find a couple of feather boas they had wrapped around themselves and tiaras that they placed on their heads. She smiled as Andrea handed her a tiara. "This one is for you."

"Thank you."

"We're going to play hide and seek. You're it," Andrea said confidently. "You have to close your eyes and count to a hundred." And with that both girls left her by herself in the hallway.

As she placed the tiara on her head, she closed her eyes and counted. In the middle of counting, she started to worry Poppy would be looking for her and peeked to see if he was coming. Seeing no one, she closed her eyes again and kept counting. When she reached one hundred, she opened them and began searching for her new friends.

There were four doors in the hallway. Two opened and two closed. She ruled out the closed bathroom door she was standing in front of, as there was no way they could have snuck past her. She took a quick look into the room with the open door, next to the bathroom, and ruled that out as it looked too adult to enter with its desk and plaques—she knew it was some sort of office room. Next to the office another open door full of dance costumes and props seemed interesting. She was instantly drawn to the colors and shapes beckoned her.

She squeezed through the dance skirts, leotards, tutus, and scarves overflowing on round racks lined side by side. She had never seen such an awesome sight and knew she wanted to be part of it. For a few moments she forgot she was looking for Marcie and Andrea until she spotted a foot sticking out from underneath one of the racks. She tiptoed to the foot and knelt down.

"I got you," she whispered as she tapped the foot. The foot moved and she heard a giggle. It was Marcie.

"How did you see me?" Marcie asked once she had gotten out from under the rack.

"Your foot."

"Oh," Marcie giggled again, grabbing her hand.

"Come on, I'll help you find Andrea."

She dragged behind as Marcie tried skipping through the hanging costumes. Once they searched the room and came up empty, they went to the only other room, which was not so much a room but a very large closet filled with mostly cleaning and office supplies. One side of the closet had deep shelves running from the bottom of the floor to the ceiling. In a matter of seconds, Marcie climbed to the top of the shelves.

Charlie followed, doing her best not to slip. She was never good at climbing trees but thought this would be a little easier. Since Andrea wasn't at the top of those shelves Marcie moved over to the next group of shelves. Soon she yelled, "I see you. You're it!" to which Andrea responded, "It doesn't count. Charlie has to get me. Charlie was it—not you!" And with apparent ease, Andrea shimmied down the shelves and headed out the door leaving Marcie and Charlie on the top shelf.

Marcie seemed to slide down easily too, while Charlie, trimmed with fear, moved more cautiously. Fear struck deep as she realized how high they were. She knew she wouldn't be able to make it down. She immediately regretted leaving Poppy in the front with Mrs. Fishkin and she froze. Marcie watched her from below.

"You remind me of a little kitty stuck in a tree!" she giggled. Then seriously she said, "Come on, you can do it, Charlie." As if trying to be helpful, she grabbed the tip of Charlie's shoe. This only made her more nervous. Panicking, she started back up the shelves, and the very foot that Marcie had touched slipped, causing her to lose balance. In a matter of seconds, she was sprawled on the floor.

"Andrea? Andrea, come here! Charlie fell!"

She cried uncontrollably, pleading, "I want Poppy," in between sobs.

Andrea ran over to Charlie, kneeling down to assess the damage. "Aw, you'll be okay. I fall all the time."

Nothing could convince Charlie that Andrea knew what she was talking about. Especially since her arm was throbbing and beginning to swell. Andrea took a look at her arm, ran out and soon returned with ice wrapped in a paper towel.

"Here, this is what my mom does when I get hurt." Andrea said as she placed the ice on Charlie's arm while Marcie made attempts to provide some comic relief. She forgot about the pain in her arm as the ice provided a soothing effect and the comedy of Marcie's slapstick, straight from the files of a Three Stooges routine, made her laugh. By the time Mrs. Fishkin found them in the closet, she was up and ready to play hide and seek again.

***

"Charlie? You listening to the doctor?"

She hasn't heard a word.

The doctor smiles and explains, "He needs a cast on his leg and that won't be able to be done until tomorrow. Besides, your grandfather's blood pressure is too high and we want him to stay overnight to get it under control."

As soon as the doctor leaves, Poppy immediately says, "We

won't be able to go home tomorrow."

"That's okay. We'll fly back when you're ready," Charlie reassures, at the same time wondering what Mr. Jimenez is going to say about her not returning to work on time.

"What was the last thing I said? Wait… that's right… I was at your mother's apartment." Poppy's face is so full of grief she wants to beg him to stop but knows she must hear the rest. He's so lost in his thoughts, minutes pass until he finally speaks.

"The door was unlocked and I went in and she was on the floor. She had taken some pills and never woke up."

By this time Poppy is inconsolable. She holds him again, reassuring him that everything is okay. All she can think about is how awful it must have been for him to find her like that and then keep it hidden for forty years.

Chapter 20
~Andrea~

"Do you want to talk about it?"

The look Chris gives Andrea as he asks reminds her of when the girls were newborns and he was afraid to hold them. He always seemed so clumsy and awkward when it came to caring for them. Now, looking back, she recognizes that he didn't want to do anything that might hurt them accidentally. She can see that now, hindsight being 20/20.

They are lying in bed and Chris is giving her that same awkward look of caution. She hasn't hardly spoken since the car ride home, only telling him a vague story about Marcie and the trip to the hospital. As he strokes her hair, she regains a renewed appreciation for him that she hasn't felt in a long time.

"I don't want to be trapped anymore, Chris."

"Trapped?" He stops stroking and says, "Do you feel trapped with me?"

As she realizes he has taken her words in the wrong context, she sits up quickly.

"No, I don't mean with you. I mean with me. I have made myself a prisoner in this house and a prisoner to myself. I have shut you all out for too long and I don't want to continue this anymore. I want to be there for you. I want to be there for our daughters."

"You're a wonderful mother and wife."

"No, I haven't been. Let's not sugarcoat this. I need to face facts. I haven't been there for you or the girls like I need to be. The other day you spoke up and told me I needed to get help. I need for you to be firm like that with me. Not all the time, mind you, but when you see that I'm getting out of control I need you to be there like that for me."

"Andrea, I will do whatever you need me to do."

"But I need you to be able to tell me what's best for me when I get to those days that I can't do that for myself. I need you to be tough on me. I need you to remind me. No more enabling."

"Are you going to bite my head off when I do?"

"Probably!"

They both snicker.

"Maybe we should come up with a code word that I can say to you. How about... flowers? You like flowers—"

"No. It needs to be something more powerful."

"Okay, how about 'red light'?"

"No, it needs to be more inspirational. How about mustard seed?"

"Mustard seed? That's a good one. 'If ye have faith as a grain of a mustard seed, ye shall say unto this mountain…'"

"Remove hence to yonder place; and it shall remove; and nothing shall be impossible for you."

"You memorized it. Andrea, I am so proud of you. What made you think of this verse?"

"When we were on our way to the hospital after the ambulance took Marcie, I was talking with Charlie. She talked me into going to the hospital and she mentioned the mustard seed. I couldn't remember that whole verse so when we were in the hospital waiting, there was a Bible on the table that I picked up. I memorized the verse while we were in there."

As she thinks of sweet Charlie, she closes her eyes and pictures the moment as if rewinding and playing back a movie.

"I can't tell you how huge this is that you made it to the hospital. Nothing is too big now, is it?"

Nodding, she opens her eyes and says, "Just a little bit at a time, though."

The familiar sound of keys opening the door downstairs interrupts their conversation and she knows Reese and Rochelle are home. Because of their busy schedules, they didn't know yet that Andrea ventured out of the house and she begged Chris not to call them. She wanted to be the one to relay the good news.

"Mom? Dad?" Reese calls upstairs.

Chris is the first to answer. "We're in the bedroom. Come here."

After several seconds of what sounds like a stampede of horses coming up the stairs, Reese and Rochelle are in the doorway and she suddenly feels anxious again. Reese seems to sense her tension and asks if she's okay.

"Yes. Please sit on the bed with us. I need to talk to both of you." Reese immediately sits down but Rochelle is more cautious and doesn't move. Andrea pats the bed.

Familiar beads of sweat linger on her forehead but she manages to take a deep breath and dive into the events of the day. When she gets to the part about actually getting into the car with Charlie, she notices both girls have their mouths wide open.

Not a word is uttered by her family as she leads them through the rest of the day and makes sure she doesn't leave any details out about the time at the hospital. She finishes up with the status of Marcie as well as Poppy, and then returning home with Chris.

Neither of the girls says a word and she wonders if it was a mistake to say anything. And then, much to her surprise, Rochelle gets up from the end of the bed and gives her a hug and quietly says, "I knew you could do it, Mom."

With her head humbly bent, she feels a hand on her shoulder and knows immediately it is Reese. "Mom, I love you so much," she whispers and she hugs the other side of her body. As Andrea holds on to both of them, she feels as if she never wants to let them go.

Chapter 21
~Marcie~

"Marcie?"

Her eyes flutter and adjust to the dim light. As they focus, Charlie's face comes into view. A few more seconds pass and she becomes disappointedly aware that she is still in the hospital.

"Come sit."

After Charlie gets settled, she grabs Marcie's hand and holds it.

"How are you feeling? Seth said you had a heart attack. I'm so sorry."

"I'm feeling better. I guess my next marathon is out of the question," she answers lightheartedly. The thought of never running another marathon, though, has her bothered.

As if reading her mind, Charlie says, "There will be other marathons for you to run." So typical of Charlie— always the encourager and voice of inspiration.

"Maybe by that time, I'll have convinced you to train with me."

"No, not me. I can't run. But you know what? Maybe I can learn to powerwalk!"

They both smile as they avoid the matter at hand. Marcie's head is still fuzzy and it's hard to figure out what to say first. Charlie beats her to it.

"I'm sorry for what happened, Marcie."

"It wasn't your fault."

"I didn't know."

"I know, Charlie. I'm not upset with you at all."

She gathers her thoughts until she finally arranges exactly what she wants to share.

"You ever feel like you're just waiting for the other shoe to drop?" Without waiting for a response, she says, "When I was little we lived in an apartment and there was a couple that lived in the apartment above us. Every Friday night they went out for their date night and they would stay out until midnight."

She feels winded and pauses. When it subsides, she continues.

"My dad would let me stay up late and usually I was still up when the couple would return to their apartment. And every time they would return, the husband would regularly drop one shoe to the ground first. It would always cause this loud thump. My father would then say, 'And soon the other shoe will drop,' and he would raise his eyebrows with a silly look of expectation on his face until the other shoe dropped. It was my sign that it was time for me to go to bed."

Charlie looks at her with a look of understanding so she keeps going.

"For my whole life it's almost like I've been waiting for that other shoe to drop since my dad died. Until I found out the whole story of his death, I couldn't move on with my life. And all of those years I must have pushed back those visions of seeing the car hit him. My mother never talked about what happened. She must have known, though."

"What a shock for you."

"And you too. I have made excuse after excuse for not doing something or worse yet for doing something that I shouldn't do as if I had a right to mess up my life. It has been my excuse my whole life. And now I don't have any more excuses because now I know the truth."

At this point, she is winded again and has to catch her breath.

"Marcie, do you need me to get the nurse?"

"No, I think I just need to be quiet for a minute."

For a couple of minutes they are quiet. Charlie finally speaks.

"I know what you mean. I felt like that with my mother. It's like I was waiting for her to walk through the door. Waiting for her to come back in my life. Waiting for something. And it never happened. Each year would bring more disappointment, more feelings of rejection. And I have based some decisions in my life on this expectation. But I don't have to wait anymore. Poppy knew that we must have discussed our childhood and he told me something I never knew. That my mother committed suicide. He's had to live with that his whole life."

Marcie is at a loss for words and is relieved when Charlie continues, "Remember the sermon that your pastor preached on David and fear? That had such a huge impact on me. The times that I've been close to God and 'in the light' were times that had nothing

141

to do with relationships… except for my relationship with Poppy. I guess that's why it was always so easy for me to wrap myself in my work. Never having to think of the things in my life that I couldn't face. Sweeping things under the rug—like my mother and intimate relationships. I don't want to be fearful anymore. And I don't want you to be fearful either."

"Me neither. And I want to start with a clean slate. I have a lot of apologies to make."

They take a break in the conversation. Marcie finally mumbles, "You've got to be exhausted. It's been a long day for you."

They say their goodbyes and the next thing Marcie knows she's alone again. Even though it's late, she knows what she must do. She searches around her bed for the phone and when she sees it, dials a number that's familiar to her. The phone seems to ring forever and she starts to hang up when she hears, "Hello?"

"Kesha? This is Marcie."

"Oh, Marcie. I didn't recognize this phone number so I almost didn't answer. Did you get a new number?"

"No, I'm in the hospital."

After Marcie tells the story and they talk about her physical state, Kesha offers get-well prayers and any assistance she can provide. Marcie then gets down to the real reason for her call.

"I need to tell you something that I have to get off my chest. I realize when I say this it will put my job in jeopardy but I can't keep living this lie and I need to ask for your forgiveness."

"Marcie, can't this hold until tomorrow? I'm sure that you need to rest and take it easy. Whatever you have to say can keep until another day."

She shakes her head. "No, this can't wait. What happened today taught me many things and one of them is that life is short and we never know when our last breath will be. I need to tell you this now. When you talked to me the other day, you asked me if I knew of any clients or staff who were using drugs illegally and who might have anything to do with Anthony. Well, I lied to you. I've been addicted to prescription drugs for a while now— probably the last couple of years. And I've been buying them through Anthony. I also…sold a few times myself."

The sigh on the other end of the phone leads Marcie to believe that Kesha is in shock from this bit of news so she is surprised to hear her say, "I suspected it for a while but I just wasn't certain. I had no proof whatsoever, but I could just tell that things hadn't been right with you and was hoping you would come around. I'm so sorry it brought you to this but God allows us to fall down to the deepest depths so that we totally reach out to him."

"This did bring me to my knees. Do you have anything new on Anthony?"

"After I helped him with bail, I was able to find him a good lawyer. He was able to go home, but it will be a long road with court. And he's going to go through some counseling too. Had you thought about what I told you?"

Puzzled, Marcie asks, "Do you mean the business card you gave me?"

"Yes."

"I do plan on calling her when I get out of the hospital. I really do want to get help. And thank you for having patience with me when I didn't deserve it."

"I'm only able to do that because of God's mercy. 'Be ye therefore merciful, as your Father is also merciful.' That's from Luke 6:36."

After they chat a while longer, Kesha hangs up with a promise of visiting the next day. A few minutes later, Seth comes in with two bags.

"What are you doing?"

Before he answers, he places both bags down on the empty chair and comes over to the bed and gives her a long kiss. She smiles and before she can thank him, he says, "I've been waiting to do that for a long time."

She's still smiling as he points to the larger bag. "Those are some clothes for me to change into. I'm sleeping over. I'll just put two comfortable hospital chairs together. And this…" he says as he grabs the smaller gift bag, "is for you."

Marcie looks at him suspiciously and then peeks into the bag. Her smile fades and once again she finds herself crying.

When they had first married, he had given her two stuffed white bears. One had a black bowtie and one a pink hair ribbon. She named them Jason and Jennifer, as a reminder of the names that they would call their children. She knows immediately why he brought them.

Seth pulls her closer and she cries into his chest. She knows this is exactly where she needs to be.

Chapter 22
~Charlie~

*B*y the time Charlie makes it back to the hotel, there is little traffic on the street and it has been dark for hours. Her feet ache and her stomach growls incessantly. She gobbles down a double cheeseburger from the closest fast food joint, certain her stomach will be paying for it later.

The Taylor paperwork is strewn about the table. Focusing on the Taylor case at this point would be moot. Her brain is too fried. She lets it wander until it lands on Poppy. After the scare at Marvin's house, maybe it's time to consider other options for him. The thought overwhelms her, and she thinks about the other two males in her life.

First she pictures Jake greeting her at the door when she returns, barely containing his excitement or his bladder. He'll do his usual routine of circling her and wagging his tale, until she scoops him up.

Jake is the best gift Lawrence has ever given her. A few years ago, on her birthday, he sent her on a scavenger hunt with clues to fun places. The last location was a pet store. As she searched for the next clue, she spotted a sign on one of the cages. A Jack Russell puppy was tumbling around inside. The sign said, "Charlie, will you take me home?" She instantly fell in love with Jake…and Lawrence.

And now the stillness of the hotel room and thoughts of the two of them make her homesick. After her nighttime routine, she calls Lawrence.

"Charlie?"

"Hi…"

"Is everything all right?"

"Yes, I'm fine. It's been a long day. I'll tell you when I see you. Right now I just need to sleep. But I do need to tell you that Poppy is in the hospital and we'll be here a little longer than expected. He broke his leg but should make a full recovery."

"How'd he do that?"

"Fell at Marvin's house. He's never broken a bone in his whole life and he does it only a couple of days after we arrive! I'll tell you about it tomorrow. How's Jake?"

"He misses you. He's been so excited when I go to feed him that he does the happy pee dance."

She smiles as Lawrence repeats a phrase that he never would have been caught dead saying if she hadn't introduced him to it.

"And don't worry—I cleaned it up."

"Thanks, Lawrence. I imagine you probably were resisting the urge to clean the rest of my house too!"

"I just straightened up a little. Is everything else okay?"

"It's fine. I'm still in shock about the Taylors. And of course Poppy. There's just so much going on. And there is something else."

"What?"

"I found out something today at Andrea's house. Something huge. Do you remember how I was telling you her mother was a hoarder? Well, she died and left Andrea a bunch of things last year. One of them was an old photo album that had a newspaper article folded inside. The article was about the accident that killed Marcie's dad. My mother was the driver."

"No way. Are you all right?"

"Yes. I needed to know the story and now I know."

Life is so fragile and unpredictable. After weeks of ups and downs and contradictions, she decides to wait to tell him about her mother's suicide; there's something more important she needs to say.

"Well, there's something else that I need to tell you too."

"What's that?"

"I love you Lawrence. I want you to know that."

He sighs and says, "I love you too. But you know that already."

And that's all she needs to hear from him. That he still loves her.

Chapter 23
~Andrea~

With the anxiety meter at its maximum level and the fight-or-flight mode almost fully engaged, Andrea pictures herself floating in a sea of mustard seeds and mountains. This vision seems to help, along with Chris by her side, and after a couple of deep breaths, she can tolerate the fifteen steps from the house to reach Charlie's rental car.

"Look at you. How's that feel to get out again?" Charlie asks, beaming ear-to-ear.

"Like heck! But I'm determined now," she answers with as much bravery as she can muster.

Chris whispers in her ear, "Are you sure you want to do this?" After she gives him a nod, he pecks her cheek and squeezes her shoulder. They exchange, "I love you" and he heads back into the house. Barely out of the driveway, Charlie gives Andrea the agenda for the morning.

"Okay, so I was thinking that we would go see Marcie first. I won't stay long so that I can be with Poppy for a little. I figured that would give you some time with Marcie by yourself. I also need to call my boss and speak to him about the Taylor case that I was telling you about. Once I'm done, I'll come back to get you. We can talk to Seth and see what we can do for them. Also, I'd like to call Mrs. Macklin sometime today so she's aware of what's going on with Poppy. Does that sound okay?"

Andrea's first impulse is to answer, "No, it doesn't." She doesn't like not being in control. No one else should be scheduling her life. It's not natural. But then thinking about the mustard seed again, she remembers God is in charge anyway. Besides, it gives her a little break.

"That will be fine," she says.

"And, Andrea, if at any time you want to leave, let me know, okay?"

"I will."

Marcie is sitting up in the chair by the hospital bed when they get there. The color has returned to her face and she almost appears to be glowing. After a group hug and morning hellos, Charlie takes off to see Poppy.

Andrea's nerves are a little jumpy but after saying a little head prayer for Marcie's sake, they settle a little.

"How are you feeling today?"

"Much better. I'm still in shock. It's like 'Wow,' this really happened to me."

Andrea nods. For once, she has nothing to say. Usually full of opinions and advice, she can't figure why her mind is blank. Maybe she's just supposed to listen.

"Andrea, I can't tell you how glad I am that you friended me on Facebook. I was explaining to Charlie that it seems like I've been waiting my whole life for yesterday, and that might not have happened if you didn't do what you did. Thank you."

"Well, I certainly never expected any of that to happen, but you're welcome."

Marcie smiles, which brings out the endearing dimples. Then she becomes serious. "I know it probably seems weird but I needed this wakeup call. I was going out of control fast. I don't know if you know this but I am addicted to painkillers. That was one of the reasons Seth and I separated. I don't know if he knew at the time the extent of my addiction, but he knew that he was married to a woman who was acting a little crazy at times!"

The similarity of their situations signals Andrea to make the next statement.

"I know what that's like."

"You do?"

"I also have some *issues*. You'll be surprised to know that I hadn't left my home in a year before yesterday. I was living like a hermit, although surrounded by my family. Yesterday's experience brought me back to reality. At least it has for the time being."

Marcie's eyes widen. "Wow! I would have never guessed that. Do you feel okay right now?"

Not holding back, she says, "Well, actually I feel like I want to run out of this hospital and go back home to hide but like Charlie told me, I'm in a good place if anything happens here."

"That's true." Marcie is silent a few seconds and then asks, "Do you mind if I ask about your mom?"

Andrea's relieved when a nurse's aide walks in with fresh water and straws. It allows a few moments to think about her question. As the nurse shuts the door she answers, "Well, I guess it depends what you want to ask."

"Do you think your mom realized it was Charlie's mom in the car?"

The question doesn't surprise Andrea. It was one she was already thinking about. Why else would she have the newspaper article hidden in the photo album? Poppy must have told her. That was the day Charlie got hurt falling off the shelves.

"Yes, I do. Poppy must have told her that day at the dance studio."

Marcie nods. "It must have been hard for her to keep that to herself for so long. My own mom never mentioned it. She must have known too."

"Yes. Secrets are like houses full of junk; eventually everything busts at the seams and needs to come out. Now it's my turn for a question."

Cocking her head, Marcie chuckles, "I feel like we're playing *truth or dare*."

"And we've skipped the dare! What happened to your mother?"

"I thought that's what you were going to ask. She still lives in Norfolk. We keep in touch but not very often. I think I remind her of my dad too much and she has never gotten over his death. Even thirty years later."

"You should do something before it's too late," Andrea says.

Marcie gives a half-smile before turning her head. Andrea realizes she's crying. She touches her shoulder. "I'm sorry, Marcie. I didn't mean anything bad by that."

"No, you're right. I know I need to talk to her more. I guess recently I've been ashamed of what I've made of myself. She expected so much more out of her one and only child. Before I see her I need to get my life straight. My boss gave me the business card of a woman she recommends at Good Tidings. Her name is Kathryn Mason."

As Marcie says the name it dawns on Andrea that this is the woman that she should talk to as well. "How about we make a pact? We both make appointments with this lady and keep each other on track to a better godly life."

"I'd like that. Maybe we should hug on it?"

As they hug, Andrea feels an extra arm wrap around her shoulders, and immediately jumps up. Charlie has returned.

"You scared the heart out of me! We need to put a bell on you!"

Charlie gives a mischievous grin that reminds her of Poppy and they all start laughing.

"Well, the bad news is that Poppy will have his surgery this afternoon and will be recovering for a little bit in Norfolk. The good news is that gives me a little more time to spend with both of you. Of course, I have to work things out with Mr. Jimenez."

"That should make Mrs. Macklin really happy that she gets to spend more time with Poppy!" Marcie teases.

"Absolutely," Charlie agrees, "And speaking of Mrs. Macklin—Marvin just picked her up and they're partying it up in the room with Poppy."

"You'll probably have to send security up there to make sure they're behaving!" Marcie pipes in again.

It's so good to see Marcie joking after her ordeal.

The morning moves quickly hanging out with Marcie. Seth joins them shortly after Charlie has returned and they get to know him better too. It is a time of healing to begin and a celebration of their renewed friendship.

With the news about Poppy's scheduled surgery, Andrea calls Chris to pick her up so Charlie doesn't need to worry about taking her home.

As they drive away from the hospital she feels so thankful she reunited with Marcie and Charlie online. She never imagined the simple act of typing a little note on the computer would bring them together in such an intimate way as to change all of their lives forever.

Let the healing begin.

Julie Kilpatrick

ABOUT THE AUTHOR

Julie Kilpatrick is a member of the Florida Writer's Association and the Jerry Jenkins Writers' Guild, and frequently helps other new authors find their writing niche.

She resides in Jacksonville, Florida with her husband, two dogs and two cats and is the grateful mother of three grown daughters who keep her mind flowing with creative ideas.